AF580962

The impure

by

John Xavier

FATHER MALACHI
(V.O.)

The Bible teaches us about evil. How we succumb to it. How to defeat it. But the meaning of its lessons aren't always clear. Take the case of Elijah and the prophets of Baal. Elijah challenged them to a trial by faith. They would each choose one bull, slaughter it, and present that offering on a pyre. Whoever's god ignited their pyre, this was the true god. So hundreds of Baal's followers agreed and danced around their offering and slashed their flesh with knives and shouted to the heavens. And Baal did nothing. "Pray louder!" taunted Elijah. "Maybe he's daydreaming or relieving himself!" After hours of this, it was Elijah's turn. So he had the people douse his sacrifice to The Lord with twelve jars of water. The pyre was completely soaked. Yet as soon as he had prayed, fire came down from the sky and consumed his entire offering. Faith had triumphed. Faith however wasn't enough. Astonished by the miracle, the huge crowd of witnesses were rendered fully obedient to Elijah and the first thing he ordered them to do was to put every prophet of Baal to death. But why? They had just witnessed The Lord's miracle. Many would no doubt have repented. Perhaps repentance, even sincere repentance, isn't good enough. That eradicating certain kinds of corruption requires something more. Ruthlessness.

CONTINUOUS:

INT. OLD BOOK STORE -- NIGHT

A man who was sitting on the floor skimming through one of the old books stands up: LUCAS D'LAMBERT (Late 20's). Slightly disheveled. Equal parts affable and cynical. He looks like someone living in the twilight between between truth and fraud.

If asked, he couldn't explain convincingly that there was any difference between these. Dressed in sombre attire.

VOICE

Found something?

LUCAS

Yeah. I think I did.

Lucas walks over to the counter where the voice is revealed to be that of the SHOPKEEPER. The shopkeeper looks at the book while they ring it up.

SHOPKEEPER

Planning on going to an exorcism? You're certainly dressed for one.

LUCAS

Funny. No. My interest in the occult's only a hobby.

SHOPKEEPER

Expensive hobby that. It'll be 68.80. Debit?

LUCAS

Yeah.

Lucas takes his purchase and exits the store.

EXT. OMINOUS DOWNTOWN STREET -- NIGHT

Lucas looks around and then crosses a road empty of traffic. He goes to a bus stop and stands there waiting. Meanwhile a man who appears to be a drug addict suffering severe psychosis is behaving strangely nearby. Tension builds. Just before it seems like something is going to happen though, the ILLUMINATED BUS arrives. Relieved, Lucas eagerly steps on board.

MATCH CUT ON DOORS:

EXT. LUCAS' APARTMENT BUILDING -- NIGHT

Lucas arrives home and fiddles in his pockets before entering. He walks upstairs and then enters his own apartment, taking less time now that he has his keys out.

INT. LUCAS' APARTMENT -- NIGHT

FEMALE VOICE

You're late.

LUCAS
(Startled)

You're not even supposed to be here.

Lucas walks into the kitchen and his girlfriend, SONJA, is waiting there (Mid 20's) She's pretty in a casual artsy way but her oversized sweater can't hide the thinness in her hands and face. Notably more mature than her romantic partner.

SONJA

The symposium ended early. The main speaker couldn't make it. Heart attack or something.

LUCAS

Shit.

There's a lull here in the conversation.

SONJA

So? How's it been?

LUCAS

Honestly? Fine.

SONJA
(Irritated)

Fine?

LUCAS

That's not what I meant.

Sonja laughs derisively. It's clear from the exchange that their relationship is not in the best shape. Lucas is acting apathetic towards Sonja and Sonja is looking for a reason to retaliate.

SONJA

You're texts haven't exactly been detailed.

LUCAS

Not a lot's been going on. Seriously. Work is… work is tedious. We're missing a lot of stuff in our inventory. The shipping and receiving guy's catching hell. Doesn't have a lot to do with me though. And I mean, other than that, things have been quiet. (Half laughs) I've just been binging movies.

A CAT comes up and rubs itself against Sonja's leg.

LUCAS
(Trying to be cheerful)

Biscuit missed you.

SONJA
(Unimpressed)

I know. He was all over me when I got home. I guess it's nice that somebody did.

Lucas doesn't know what to say. He approaches SONJA ambiguously and then reaches past her into a cupboard.

LUCAS

I didn't have a chance to go grocery shopping. But I was thinking pasta?

SONJA

I already ate.

LUCAS

Oh. Okay.

After an awkward moment, SONJA leaves and Lucas pauses, obviously thinking about the conversation that just happened. Then he continues with making dinner.

VIEW ON LUCAS FINISHING UP IN THE KITCHEN

Lucas has a bowl of noodles he is pouring sauce over.

LUCAS

"Après moi, le déluge."

INT. LIVING ROOM -- NIGHT

Lucas enters with his food and sits down beside Sonja on a couch. A black and white movie is playing on TV. Sonja stares at Lucas for a few seconds as he obliviously focuses on his food. Finally a look of disgust passes over her face and she gets up.

SONJA

I'm tired. I'm going to bed.

LUCAS

Alright. I'm just going to finish this and I'll probably join you.

SONJA
(Slightly sarcastic)

Yeah?

Sonja exits and Lucas returns to his meal. As he's eating though, something starts to disturb him. It's the movie on TV. An old black and white picture, vaguely surrealist, with a woman being chased by a vague antagonist through long, poorly lit corridors. The woman silently shouts at her pursuer but no sound is heard. Lucas frowns and reaches for the REMOTE where increasing the volume does nothing. Getting up he goes to the TV to fix it. Just before he touches it, and just as the woman in the movie is about to be overcome, the TV screen turns to static and the loud accompanying NOISE causes Lucas to wince. The shot lingers on the noise and his distress.

DISSOLVE TO:

CLOSE IN ON LUCAS' DISHES IN THE SINK.

The tap is DRIPPING. Otherwise quiet.

INT. BEDROOM -- NIGHT

Lucas enters with the book he bought as Sonja is checking her PHONE. He's changed into an underwear and t-shirt combo and gets in bed beside her. While he's settling in, Sonja quickly puts a sleeping VISOR on and turns away from him. Lucas hesitates before saying something.

LUCAS
(Whispering)

Do you mind if I read for a bit?

Receiving no answer, Lucas shrugs and opens his book. FLIPPING through the pages he comes across a SLIP OF PAPER inserted inside with a printed poem that captures his attention.

INSERT POEM

ENOCH
(V.O.)

Lost Immortals

The starlight of the empty eons,
The dust of unburied bones;
A black lake of volcanic ash,
Poison berries along the road

Fog and mist the entire journey,
Pale the reproach of a lonely moon;
Every village just a graveyard,
Every castle a musty tomb

And we remain good pilgrims,
Faithful despite our father's fall;
Those surviving off his vineyard,
Darkness shielding us from awe

CONTINUOUS:

Lucas sitting in bed. Furrows brow before turning off the lamp.

SNAP TO BLACK:

INT. LUCAS' APARTMENT -- NIGHT

HALLWAY

Lucas is walking down the hall with a perplexed look on his face. TRACKING on Lucas as he enters the bathroom.

BATHROOM

Lucas looks over and notices that the bathtub is full. Focus on Lucas as he approaches and his facial expressions. These go from confusion to shock.

MEDIUM SHOT OF BATHTUB

The clear water is full of hundreds of leeches. Anxiety inducing synth sounds play in a swelling instrumental.

CLOSE IN ON LEECHES

They wriggle as they swim. Searching for blood.

EXTREME CLOSE IN

The details of the leeches.

CUT TO BLACK:

Silence. Then the annoying ALERT of a digital alarm clock. Lucas is heard grumbling and shutting off the alarm.

EXT. AUTO REPAIR SHOP -- DAY

Noise of the WORK going on inside and light TRAFFIC sounds.

INT. AUTO REPAIR SHOP -- DAY

Lucas, in overalls, is working on a motorcycle. He's fully concentrating on fixing the machine when another co-worker walks up to him. It's WERNER "Vern" GAUSS (Late 50s) the senior mechanic. He has the quality of an old hunting dog about him. Capable and unrushed.

WERNER

You're missing your break.

Lucas looks up.

VIEW ON WALL CLOCK

LUCAS

Ah. Thanks Vern.

Lucas wipes his hands off with a rag and gets to his feet. After looking around for a few seconds to make sure he isn't forgetting anything, Lucas exits the auto repair shop.

EXT. BEHIND AUTO REPAIR SHOP -- DAY

Lucas sees that another one of his coworkers, ROYCE (30s) is already loitering there, CHEWING gum and looking at his PHONE. Lucas walks a little ways away and takes out his own PHONE.

LUCAS
(Making a call)

Hi. This is Lucas D'Lambert. Yeah. I'm the guy who emailed you about the poem. Oh, nothing like that. No. I mean, it interests me. Sure. I've written a couple things online. Yeah. Nothing too prestigious (Laughs) Right. So I was hoping you could connect me with the publisher. (Two beats) I don't even know yet. More curiosity. I know. I know. (Long pause and Lucas fidgets) Of course. I understand. But if he hasn't been in contact with you for ten years… really? Yeah. If it's been that long, I could do you a favor. I'll check in on him. And pass that information along. (Two beats) Great. I'll be totally discrete. Okay. Yep. Talk to you soon. Bye.

Lucas is visibly satisfied with himself for a moment.

VIEW ON ROYCE

ROYCE

(Sneering and chewing gum)

Not enough to do what we do, eh Lamby?

WIDE SHOT OF BOTH MEN

LUCAS

Maybe your focus could be better spent looking for those parts Royce?

ROYCE
(Simmering with hostility while still chewing)

Maybe you don't got to worry about that.

LUCAS
(Decisively)

Maybe it shouldn't have even happened.

Lucas walks out of sight.

CLOSE UP OF ROYCE

A look of absolute fury on Royce's face. He's stopped chewing.

DISSOLVE TO:

INT. AUTO REPAIR SHOP -- EVENING

End of work hours. Lucas and Werner are cleaning up.

WERNER

I think I owe you a drink from last week.

LUCAS
(Smiling)

Thanks Vern. Tomorrow though. I've gotta run.

WERNER

That girl of yours? (Thinking) Sonja?

LUCAS

(Laughs) Actually I've got to go see this antiquarian. Part of a writing project I've been working on.

Werner arches an eyebrow as he hauls a bag of garbage out of a trash can. He pauses to eye Lucas carefully.

WERNER

You have to go after the things you want in life. And, if you're lucky, you'll find out what's truly important to you before it's too late.

Werner leaves with a nod and Lucas watches him go.

EXT. ENOCH'S HOUSE -- EVENING

WIDE SHOT

An older home with a run-down quality to it. A garden that's become wild through neglect out front and a large porch with various pieces of JUNK on it.

Lucas approaches, walking right up to the front door, after opening the OUTER GLASS DOOR, and knocking on it. Then he lets the glass door close shut.

CLOSE IN AND PENDULUM PAN

Lucas is waiting for an answer when a white dove settles nearby. Distracted, he doesn't notice when the occupant of the house arrives at the door window and stares at him. This is ENOCH KOLMOGOROV (Late 60s) an antiquarian. Enoch is a grim figure who has a rather unsettling quality about him. And yet he has old fashioned manners and often attempts to engage in pleasantries.

ENOCH
(As he opens the inner door)

Who are you?

LUCAS
(Surprised)

Oh. Mr. Kolmogorov? I'm Lucas. Lucas D'Lambert.

ENOCH

And what do you want?

LUCAS

You were partners with Charles Poole. I mean, um, I contacted him about a book you published: Esoteric Traditions in Early Medieval Society. I was curious about a poem I found in it.

ENOCH

There wasn't any poetry in that.

LUCAS

It was on a slip of paper I found in one of the editions.

ENOCH

Why would you think I'd know anything about some random…

LUCAS

The starlight of the empty eons?

Enoch frowns. Clearly he's familiar with the poem.

ENOCH
(Suspicious)

Who are you with?

Now it's Lucas' turn to frown and he glances behind him to see if Enoch is referring to anyone in particular before answering.

LUCAS

With? This is my own personal thing.

Enoch rubs his face as he thinks. Then he pushes open the glass door. Lucas grabs this to hold it open, unsure of what Enoch is intending though.

ENOCH
(Nodding to indicate a spot)

Take your shoes off and put 'em over there.

Enoch vanishes into the house and Lucas follows after a moment of hesitation.

INT. ENOCH'S HOUSE - LIVING ROOM -- EVENING

The décor is practically late Victorian. An absurd amount of ASSORTED ANIMAL TAXIDERMY fills the room. Lucas, sitting in a chair, eyes one of these creations warily before turning towards Enoch, also in a chair.

LUCAS

So? Can you tell me who wrote it?

Enoch lights a cigarette.

ENOCH

No. It's an anonymous work. What's your interest in it?

LUCAS

The last stanza. The fallen father is a reference to Adam presumably. But my own studies connects this with… with the Lucifer mythos. With Satan.

ENOCH

And those are two different individuals?

LUCAS

Well, Lucifer and Satan…

ENOCH
(Interrupting)

Lucifer and Adam.

Lucas doesn't know what to make of this suggestion. Enoch takes a long drag from his cigarette.

ENOCH

The clay is just a vessel.

VIEW ON ENOCH

He is staring at Lucas very intently. At a certain point though he seems to relent.

ENOCH

I found it written in Armenian with an accompanying English translation. The poem. This was at a booksellers in Ephesus.

LUCAS

And… no attribution?

Enoch stubs out his cigarette.

ENOCH

I assumed the translation was Byron at first. No proof either way though.

LUCAS
(Eyes widening)

Really? (Beat) And the original?

ENOCH
(Weighing his words)

Much older.

WIDE SHOT

The two men facing each other. Nothing happening.

ENOCH

(Insinuating)

You know what they say about curiosity and felines.

Lucas turns to look at one of the preserved animals. A CAT.

CLOSE IN ON CAT THEN CUT TO MEDIUM SHOT OF LUCAS

LUCAS
(With a sly grin)

No. Not really. But I'm definitely interested in finding out.

Enoch chuckles, pauses, and then chuckles again.

DISSOLVE TO:

INT. ENOCH'S HOUSE - LIBRARY -- NIGHT

Enoch enters first, then Lucas. The former has been giving the latter a tour of the house.

ENOCH

It's hardly what it used to be but this is what remains.

Enoch gestures to a wall of shelves overflowing with old books.

LUCAS

Wow. It's still very impressive. How many?

ENOCH

Just over three thousand. Less than half. In the last move… there were complications.

LUCAS
(Confused)

Do you… move often?

Enoch idly takes a book down and examines it.

ENOCH
(Almost to himself)

Like rain driving up the worms. (Beat) Here.

Enoch hands Lucas the book he was holding.

ENOCH

You'll need a few more too.

Lucas is surprised. He wasn't expecting to receive any books. Meanwhile Enoch thoughtfully goes through his library and pulls out various HARDCOVER VOLUMES. When Enoch finishes, Lucas is holding a considerable stack of books and straining somewhat as a result of this.

ENOCH

How's that?

CLOSE IN ON LUCAS' FACE AND UPPER TORSO

LUCAS

Uh. (Beat) Could I borrow a bag?

Enoch gestures for Lucas to follow him.

DISSOLVE TO:

INT. ENOCH'S HOUSE - FOYER -- NIGHT

Lucas has been given a SMALL DUFFLE BAG to carry the books in. Enoch follows him to the door with a cup of tea.

LUCAS

I really appreciate all this Mr. Kolmogorov. I'll email you when I finish the article.

ENOCH

I look forward to reading it. You sure the busses are still running?

LUCAS

Yeah. I mean, as far as I know.

ENOCH

Alright. We'll talk again soon Lucas.

Enoch opens the interior door. Lucas opens the exterior one.

LUCAS

Absolutely. And thank you. Again. This means a lot to me.

Enoch waves off Lucas' gratitude and Lucas raises his hand as he departs. Enoch watches him for a moment. There's an unexpected cheerlessness in his face though.

TRACK Enoch as he returns to the living room. His movements are slow. Subdued. His age is noticeable. He grabs a package he received when he gets there and places it on a dining table. He then scrounges for a box-cutter in a drawer and sits down. Camera follows as he carefully slices the package open with neat cuts. After finishing he deliberately places the knife down.

WIDE SHOT

Enoch is still sitting at the dining table but now the full menagerie of animal taxidermy is visible. Enoch seems disturbed. He stops. Listening. Then suddenly he tries to grab the box-cutters again. Before he can though, a statue-like figure clad in black, barely noticeable among all the dead animals, comes at him from behind and stabs Enoch in the heart.

CLOSE IN

Enoch and his killer.

ASSASSIN
(Whispering)

So close.

The ASSASSIN, large and disguised in a CUSTOM BALACLAVA, holds Enoch's arms with one of his own while brutally jostling his knife in the wound. Enoch writhes in pain, starts gasping, and finally dies. His eyes and mouth remain open as the Assassin lets him go and departs. Camera lingers on Enoch's dead body.

CUT TO:

INT. AUTO REPAIR SHOP -- EARLY MORNING

LIGHT is streaming in through the windows. A few dust particles dance in the air. After the camera briefly surveys the details of the room, Lucas enters the frame and busies himself with some organizational tasks. Entirely relaxed, the movement of the camera emphasizes his mood but there's a growing tension in the scene that plays out on Lucas' face before he finally decides to listen to a VOICEMAIL that he'd received hours ago. As he holds the phone to his ear, the voicemail plays.

CHARLES POOLE
(V.O.)

Lucas? This is Charles Poole. We spoke the other day. I'm… I'm sorry. I'm just in shock at the moment. A colleague of mine's insisting that Enoch (?)died(?) yesterday. Ah, I'm trying to get some more details but there's nothing in the news. Did you speak with him? I mean, maybe you're already in contact with the police. I'd… uh… appreciate it if you can call me though. For some reason I, I don't want to believe this. Um… I'll be in the office in an hour or so. Get in touch with me as soon as you can. Thank you.

After listening to the voicemail, Lucas pauses in stunned silence. He exhales quietly. His posture deflates. Eventually, after holding his forehead as if he has an oncoming headache, Lucas dials Charles Poole's office.

LUCAS

Hi. This is Lucas D'Lambert. I'm calling for Mr. Poole. (Three beats) No, no. You mean Mr. Kolmogorov right? (Beat) Him also? I mean, uh… both of them? Wow… how? But you're not saying they were in the same car. That's… Just Mr. Poole? Okay but then… What! Um, how? Uh, how-how do they know it was a… murder. But, uh… well, I was going to speak to Mr. Poole because… (Long pause) Yeah (Slowly) I'm still here. You know what, I uh… I think this is a bad time. Yeah. I'm… I'm sorry. No, no. No, I appreciate your help. Yeah. You too. (Beat) Goodbye.

Lucas is thoroughly distressed and disoriented now. Stumbling to make his way over to a stool, Lucas slumps down on it and stares off into space. Open to a wide shot to impress his isolation.

EXT. AUTO REPAIR SHOP -- DAY

Werner and Royce are outside smoking together. The sense we get of their relationship from body language is that Royce is reluctantly deferential towards Werner and that neither has any special affection for the other. They can work together in an effective manner but they're not friends. This is also why Royce resents Lucas, a newer hire than himself, establishing a genuinely good relationship with the senior mechanic.

Royce, casually tosses a cigarette butt on the ground and then looks over at Werner.

ROYCE

The tires for the YAMAHA should arrive by express courier today. I can call the owner up once they do right?

WERNER
(Dropping a butt in a tin)

Well, Lucas is the one working on that. (Scoffs) Not me. But, yeah, he's done everything else as far as I know. Just give him time to put the new tires on before the owner gets here, okay?

ROYCE
(Making a sour face)

Of course.

The two men head inside the building.

INT. AUTO REPAIR SHOP -- DAY

Werner and Royce enter more or less in succession and are getting ready to go over some business with Lucas when Werner notices that something seems wrong.

WERNER
(Trying to be lighthearted)

Hey? You alright there kid?

Lucas looks up from his hands. There's an obvious bleakness in his eyes and an aura of trepidation around him.

LUCAS

Vern. I'm… no.

Puzzled looks from both Werner and Royce. Softly in the former, suspiciously in the latter.

LUCAS

Someone I know, someone I knew, is dead.

WERNER
(Gently)

Someone you were close to?

LUCAS
(Slightly surprised)

No. It's not that.

All three men are silent. Almost like a Mexican standoff, no one ready to make the first move. Finally, Lucas gets up from his stool but accidentally knocks it over trying to push it aside.

LUCAS
(Said in epiphany)

I've… I can't be here. I need to leave.

Hearing this, Royce scowls in disbelief.

ROYCE
(With rising anger)

What! You're going to go and fuck us like this? You don't think we don't have our own fucking problems? My cousin died three months ago! Remember? I still came into work! What are you?

LUCAS
(Groping for words)

I'm sorry.

ROYCE
(Furious)

You're more than sorry. You're pathetic.

WERNER
(In rebuke)

Hey!

Werner and Royce exchange an intense stare before Lucas interrupts by weakly waving for their attention.

LUCAS

I'll just be gone for a while. Okay?

Lucas hesitates and then barrels out of the room. Royce melodramatically recoils in disgust while Werner tries to put a consoling hand on Lucas during the latter's exit.

WERNER

Lucas…

With Lucas' departure, a tense silence settles in. Royce gestures and gives Werner a pointed look like "Is this the way things are now?"

CUT TO:

EXT. URBAN NEIGHBORHOOD -- DAY

A street of cookie-cutter houses in a working class area of the city. Shots of local traffic and diverse representatives of the local population. Focus finally on one of the unexceptional homes. Dolly shot through the front gate and along the side of the house until coming to the entrance of a basement suite. Close in on Lucas' hand as it knocks on the door. Widen to Lucas in profile, wearing a JACKET and waiting at the door.

Finally, SAMMY emerges; low-level middle-age drug dealer living in a basement suite. He's wearing a wife beater, sweat pants, and a pair of sandals. Distinctly unhealthy looking as well as obviously not being someone who exercises regularly.

SAMMY
(Sternly)

What are you doing here?

LUCAS
(Tiredly)

Come on man.

SAMMY
(Confrontational)

No. You think you can just show up at my door in the middle of the day? Like you don't have to call first?

LUCAS
(Exasperated)

Look. Not today. Please.

Sammy eyes Lucas a moment before dropping the façade.

SAMMY

Heh. Alright. Allll-right…

Sammy gestures for Lucas to enter. Lucas does and Sammy lingers in the doorway curiously before following.

CUT TO:

INT. SAMMY'S BASEMENT SUITE -- DAY

The place is a somewhat typical bachelor sty full of empty liquor bottles, drug paraphernalia, and random items in bad taste. Notable though is a small CRYPTO MINING RIG. Lucas and Sammy sit down on a couch.

SAMMY

So what? You just here to pick up?

LUCAS

(Sighs) What I need is to take my mind off some shit for a minute. (Shakes head) You good if I only score a blunt off you?

Lucas pulls out a folded TEN DOLLAR BILL between his thumb and index fingers with a slightly penitent look on his face.

SAMMY

Yeah, I got you. (Snatches the money) You know I got you bruh.

LUCAS

Thanks. If you can… roll it too…

SAMMY
(Feigning indignation)

(Laughs) This guy… actin' the heavy, bangin' on my door… barge-ING in, bosssin' me around. Fuck.

LUCAS

I mean, you know, I was gonna smoke it with you. You wanna risk me rollin' it?

Sammy gives Lucas a blank stare before busting into laughter.

SAMMY

Hellll nah. You can't roll worth shit. (Laughs) But that's okay. That's fine. I'm the fuckin' Leon of this life. Pro-fessional. Yer local gold standard. Rolled gold. Eyyy? Rolllled goaled. (Beat) Watch and learn son.

Sammy deftly rolls the BLUNT without the aid of a table before showing it off in an exaggerated manner and then tossing it at Lucas with theatrical indifference. Caught off guard, Lucas still manages to catch it and proceeds to examine it for damage.

SAMMY

Go on. Spark that shit. Clock's ticking Gretzky.

After hitting Sammy with a bemused/nonplussed look, Lucas proceeds to do as he's asked, grabbing a LIGHTER off the LIVING ROOM TABLE in turn. Once he's had a few tokes from the blunt, he hands it off to Sammy who wastes no time in partaking as well.

SAMMY

You know I don't let just anybody chill at my place right?

LUCAS

I know.

SAMMY
(After handing off blunt)

Cause, yo, that's some dumb shit. Randoms in the crib… it's a recipe for fucking problems. Ungrateful motherfuckers gettin' a mind to rip you off and shit. (Receives blunt back and tokes) You're one of my best customers though Luke. (Takes another hit) Luke Nukem. (Exhales smoke)

LUCAS
(Rolling his eyes)

Thanks.

SAMMY

Hey bruh. I'm an appreciative dude. (Checks a text on his phone before ignoring it and getting handed the blunt again) Not every customer's a good one. Fuck. Next to my bitcoin pump, yer my most reliable source of income. (Laughs)

Lucas has notably loosened up now. He grins while quickly glancing at the crypto mining setup.

LUCAS

I don't know if I can handle all these compliments. (Laughs)

Sammy laughs again and the two finish the blunt halfway before Lucas decides he's had enough. Instead of toking he gestures wordlessly towards Sammy with the blunt and the latter shakes his head to decline. Lucas then stubs it out.

LUCAS

Hey. I gotta piss.

SAMMY
(Gesturing to the washroom)

Me casa eh tu casa

Sammy's butchered attempt at Spanish goes unremarked as Lucas gets up and steps inside the bathroom, the view from the outer hall continuing as the door is respectfully shut. Hold shot as noise and muffled speech from Sammy continue.

INSIDE BATHROOM

Lucas finishes urinating with the toilet seat up. After he's done he puts the toilet seat down out of habit then, following an indecisive moment of reconsideration, he puts it back up. Goes to wash his hands and stares at himself in the mirror. Some of the energy drains out of him for a moment. He rubs his face with both hands. Flash an insert of the mirror without his reflection in it. His hands fall from his face. He opens his eyes. He looks at himself again and resolve now returns to his expression. He turns away.

OUTSIDE BATHROOM

Hallway adjacent to bathroom. Lucas opens the door and exits. Turns off the light before leaving. TRACK backwards as Lucas walks towards the room where Sammy is waiting. Sammy is standing and has two BEERS in his hands. Offers one to Lucas who accepts.

SAMMY

Yo. Check these prank highlights out. (Laughs)

LUCAS

Oh?

The two men sit down on a couch in front of Sammy's LAPTOP.

CUT TO:

EXT. DEAD END ALLEY -- DAY

A long shot parallel-center down the alley as a man walks out of a backdoor from left of frame. He's dressed in grim business attire. As he heads towards the camera he notices another man slumped over on the right side of the frame. Disheveled and homeless apparently. Just as the business man passes the homeless man though he sees a dozen or so TWENTY DOLLAR BILLS scattered in the street. As he stoops down to inspect these, the homeless man suddenly comes to life and stealthily rushes the business man with a KNIFE. The assassin now begins to stab the VICTIM repeatedly as heavy ominous music swells in, drowning out the noise of the attack. The shot holds as the victim is stabbed in a brutally lopsided fight. Eventually they succumb to this and the assassin finishes by slitting their throat and then briskly walking away. As they near the camera, we get the sense that this is the assassin who killed Enoch due to the same balaclava each are wearing. After the assassin exits the frame, the shot remains on the still body of the murder victim.

The noise of ordinary street traffic returns.

CUT TO:

INT. SAMMY'S BASEMENT SUITE -- EVENING

Sammy and Lucas are still enjoying themselves. They're playing a fighting game on a GAME CONSOLE and engaging in some light banter. After a match, Sammy gets up from the couch to grab something to eat.

SAMMY
(Joking)

I can't believe I lost again to someone as terrible as you.

LUCAS
(Amused)

You'll never live it down.

Sammy returns with a bag of JERKY and watches as Lucas starts a match with the computer.

SAMMY

Well, I'm still ahead what? Ten games to three?

LUCAS
(Grimacing)

Something like that. Fuck. At least it's better than dying in real life.

SAMMY
(Stops eating)

Huh?

LUCAS
(Attention fixed on game)

Yeah, uh, today was crazy. Two people I spoke with died today. I mean I didn't really know either of them. But…

SAMMY

Seriously?

LUCAS
(Attention still fixed on game)

Honest. I uh, went to this one guy's house, older guy, to talk to him about a book. Well, yeah, kind of. But apparently he died the day I met him. Stabbed. Like soon after I left. And then the guy who I called to get his address died in a car crash too. I got the news at work today and, fuck, a wave of paranoia hit me. I don't know. I mean if anything's going on there I'm not involved in it but, the police are probably gonna call me at some point right? The whole thing's a mess.

SAMMY
(Livid)

Are you fucking stupid?

LUCAS
(Turning to Sammy in surprise)

Bro, it's not…

SAMMY
(Yelling)

You're a murder suspect!

Fear creeps in to Lucas' expression as he realizes that Sammy is right. Sammy supresses an animalistic scream.

SAMMY
(Struggling to keep his voice down)

Holy fuck! You were the last person to see someone who got fucking stabbed to death! Or maybe not but you're still the prime fucking suspect! There's the fucking phone records "bruh"! And transit surveillance "bruh"! Right!? And what the fuck do you do!? Oh my god! You decided to come hang out with your fucking drug dealer! I mean, whattttt thhhhe fuckkk! (Beat) FFFFUCK!!!

LUCAS
(Worried)

It's not like…

SAMMY
(Seething)

SHUT UP! Shut the fuck up! Oh my god, oh MY god. How can you not understand what the fuck you just did!?

Lucas gives Sammy a sickly look.

SAMMY

What do you think the police DO when someone gets murdered!? They fucking track the killer down!!! They fucking identify everyone who had any fucking contact with the dumb fuck who just DIED and interrogate their fucking asses. And you, YOU FUCKING CUNT, decided to drag me into this shit! You cause you're SOOOO fucking innocent! Con-Gratulations. Halle-fucking-looya! It's not like innocent people ever go to jail. It's not like some murder detective with a desperate fucking HARD-ON for closing a major case isn't going to put the fucking screws to any dipshit unlucky enough to get within a hundred feet of a dead body. Never mind the fact that they'll slam me with any number of fucking real charges and trumped-up bullshit just to squeeze whatever they can out of me!

LUCAS
(Miserably)

I'm sorry. I wasn't thinking.

SAMMY

Get out. Get out of my fucking house! And don't fucking mention this idiotic visit to any fucking cops. And don't fucking call me! And don't fucking say anything! To anyone!

CUT TO:

EXT. SAMMY'S BASEMENT SUITE -- EVENING

Lucas is pushed out with his JACKET in his hands. The camera, parallel with the side of the house, can't see inside but we can hear Sammy bang the door shut after him. With a rueful face, Lucas begins to leave the property.

CUT TO:

EXT. 1ST RESIDENTIAL NEIGHBORHOOD -- EVENING

Lucas, wearing JACKET, arrives at a bus stop with some other BUS RIDERS and stands waiting. Then, thinking about it, he changes his mind and leaves. What Sammy said earlier about transit surveillance has convinced him to walk home. Hold shot with the other people still waiting for the bus.

CUT TO:

A montage of Lucas walking alone on his way home. It's clear he's wrestling with his thoughts while simultaneously worrying about the possibility of police around him. Use diminishing light to convey passage of time.

CUT TO:

EXT. 2ND RESIDENTIAL NEIGHBORHOOD -- NIGHT

EXTREME WIDE SHOT

Rear view of a POLICE CAR slowly cruising along a major street. Slow ZOOM in and PAN on Lucas farther ahead as he notices the police approaching.

CLOSER IN BUT STILL WIDE

Lucas panics before exiting right of frame into a side street.

CUT TO:

EXT. ADJACENT ALLEY -- NIGHT

Lucas enters the alley, looking over his shoulder once, and then creeps up to a wall along the left side of the frame. Time passes as he waits to see if the police follow him in. He prepares to run for it but no police show up. After a few more seconds he cautiously begins to walk up the alley.

CLOSE IN AND DOWNWARD 45 DEGREE ANGLE

Lucas walking through the alley. He passes under the bright light of a tall lamppost but after a few seconds a rapid SHADOW briefly sweeps over him. Startled, he turns around.

EXTREME CLOSE IN

A HAND GUN, a Beretta 9mm or something similar, held in a WEAVER STANCE by expert hands. Hold shot as their owner begins to talk.

UMBERTO
(With sinister calm)

At this range you might think a bullet would go right through you but actually it'll only penetrate your skull once. Then the bullet will spin and ricochet inside your head. …

CLOSE IN

Umberto is smiling with full teeth. He's a very formidable looking man with strong Mediterranean features. Like an émigré gangster or mercenary.

UMBERTO
(Enjoying himself)

… Burrowing tunnels in your brains. Turning them to mush. And you're dumb enough as it is.

LUCAS
(Flinching)

Plea-eeze d-don't…

Umberto raises a finger to his own lips.

UMBERTO
(Shushing Lucas)

Shhhhhhhhh.

Umberto slowly lowers his finger and resumes a cool grip on his pistol with both hands. The shot holds on both of them. Umberto eyes Lucas with something nearly like indifference while Lucas shivers in adrenaline pulsing fright. Finally a UTILITY VAN rushes towards them and stops.

SWITCH TO A LONG SHOT

Umberto grabs Lucas by the neck and, along with two KIDNAPPERS who appear from the side door of the van, has a HOOD forced on Lucas before pushing him inside. Then the van speeds away.

CUT TO:

EXT. AERIAL VIEW OF THE DOWNTOWN -- NIGHT

Sounds of the van racing through traffic. Jostling and thuds from those in the back. Noise of other cars. Emphasize the tension of being kidnapped. Continue for several seconds.

UMBERTO
(V.O.)

Almost there.

DISSOLVE TO:

INT. UNDERGROUND PARKING LOT

First person view from Lucas's perspective, except he's still in the hood so only the light leaking through its fabric is visible as he's pushed out of the van and then hung upside-down on a CONTRAPTION. When the hood is removed, the VIEW IS UPSIDE-DOWN with just the legs of those in front of him visible. For the most part these are the pant legs of his male kidnappers. One pair of legs though reveals the pale skin of a beautiful woman wearing a RED EVENING DRESS that ends just above the knee line.

VIEW ON LUCAS' FACE

He's blinking and looking around as his eyes adjust to the light. Finally he settles on the lone woman in front of him.

VIEW ON KIDNAPPERS

Standing among Umberto and three other kidnappers is ADRIENNE, a cold blooded femme fatale (Early 30's) who is as meticulous in her speech as she is in her appearance. She moves carefully, like a snake sensing heat in the air from nearby prey.

ADRIENNE
(Gently)

Where are you Lucas?

LUCAS
(Terrified)

I… I don't know.

ADRIENNE

(Delicately)

Yes. And none of your friends or family know where you are either. Which means it's very easy for you to (Soft gesture) disappear.

LUCAS
(Pleading)

I'm innocent. (Stress "innocent" with a whine)

ADRIENNE
(Bemused)

What does that have to do with anything?

VIEW ON LUCAS

Lucas' eyes shift between the other people present.

ORGANIC VIEW ON KIDNAPPERS UPSIDE-DOWN

Their faces are all made of stone. Successive close ups of each, still upside-down and looking at camera, to punctuate this.

ADRIENNE
(Thoughtfully)

Perhaps I should clarify some things. We know you met with Enoch just before his death. We also know you wanted to speak to him about a book he wrote. (Raises eyebrows)

LUCAS
(Wincing)

And?

ADRIENNE

Why did he die Lucas?

LUCAS
(Begging)

I had nothing to do with it. Really.

ADRIENNE

So you don't know anything?

LUCAS

I… don't think so.

VIEW ON KIDNAPPERS

Umberto can no longer hold back his exasperation and so he gets down on one knee before grabbing Lucas by the hair and forcing him to look below. It becomes evident now that Lucas has his hands HANDCUFFED behind his back so he offers little resistance.

VIEW ON LUCAS' FACE AND THE GROUND BELOW HIM

A METAL CONTAINER is sitting underneath Lucas as he hyper-ventilates and writhes in response to Umberto's manhandling.

UMBERTO
(Irritated)

See that? Look at it. (Beat) Do you know how much liquid that can hold?

Umberto pulls out a KNIFE and draws it near Lucas' throat.

UMBERTO

Twice as much as what's in you.

LUCAS struggles, grunting and moaning.

ADRIENNE
(Encouragingly)

It doesn't have to be this way Lucas. Just tell us what happened.

LUCAS
(Breathing frantically)

I… I got his address from Obscura publishing. From, uh, Mr. Laird. But he's dead too!

ADRIENNE

(Half mischievous, half bored)

We're aware.

Adrienne gestures for Lucas to continue

LUCAS
(Babbling)

Okay. Alright. So I, uh, go to his place right? A house. Full of dead animals. I uh, I uh, I tell him I'm interested in his book. Esoteric Traditions in, um… ah… you know the one? The… anyway, but it's not the book specifically. Right. There was uhhh… a poem, yeah, in the book I bought. Scrap paper.

ADRIENNE
(Frowning slightly)

A poem?

LUCAS

Yeah. Lost… Immortals!

ADRIENNE
(Amused and nodding)

Oh. That poem.

LUCAS

So you know? Of course. But, ah, we didn't, ah, discuss it too much. I just wanted to write an article, I was going to write an article. On the symbolism. That's all. And, uh, and he said he'd help me. Well, he uh, he gave me some books. Just books. For research.

FOCUS ON UMBERTO, STILL CROUCHING

UMBERTO
(To Adrienne)

It doesn't sound like he knows anything.

Adrienne shrugs, terrifying Lucas.

LUCAS
(Glancing between Adrienne and Umberto)

Wait! WAIT! I'll help! Anything! I'll do whatever I can. I'll help however. Just, just, just…

Umberto looks questioningly at Adrienne. After giving it a moment's thought, she gestures for Umberto to stand up.

ADRIENNE

Who knows? We might find a use for him.

LUCAS
(Relieved and grateful)

YES. THANK YOU. I-I promise you won't regret it.

CLOSE IN ON LUCAS

He is taken by surprise as Umberto pulls a hood up over his face again and cinches it with draw strings around his neck.

FADE TO:

EXT. CITY SCENERY -- NIGHT

The streets are pervaded with menace. Include a shot of a rat investigating the body of a man passed out on pavement. Focus on garbage and grime while juxtaposing this with corporate architecture. The darkness is omnivorous.

FATHER MALACHI
(V.O.)

Evil cannot live on its own; it thrives on the vitality of others and, the more power it obtains, the more monstrous it becomes. Its own industry and labor are abhorrent to it so it enslaves and perverts those it can to bend them to subservience. Like a poison root, it spreads through the land, destroying whatever soil it touches. It's not enough then to eradicate evil in its expression. This is like pruning the flowers of a weed in the hope of halting its expansion. To truly destroy evil we must destroy everything infected with it, everything polluted by abomination. Without the handicaps of mercy. Even a single drop of tainted blood can unleash the horrors of plague.

CUT TO:

EXT. LUCAS' NEIGHBORHOOD -- NIGHT

The van with Lucas and his kidnappers arrives into frame from around a corner and slows down.

UMBERTO
(V.O.)

Quite a night, eh Lucas? You're alive, for a little while longer at least. Of course you understand this is a matter of our discretion right? (With incredible menace) Because I'll fucking kill you if you try anything stupid. And not just you. Sonja. Your parents. Whoever you care about most. Got it?

CUT TO:

INT. KIDNAPPER'S VAN -- NIGHT

Lucas is being held around the neck by KIDNAPPER 1 with his hood still on. Not receiving a response to his question, Umberto leans over and snatches the hood off.

UMBERTO

Well?

LUCAS
(With closed eyes)

Yes. Yes.

UMBERTO
(Satisfied)

Alright. (Looking at KIDNAPPER 2) Grab his phone from the Faraday cage. (Looking at the phone after being handed it) Uh oh. I don't think your girlfriend's going to appreciate that you've been ducking her calls. Good luck with that.

The van stops and Kidnapper 2 opens the door while Kidnapper 1 pushes Lucas out.

CUT TO:

EXT. LUCAS' NEIGHBORHOOD -- NIGHT

Lucas stumbles out of the van with his phone in his hand. He stands there unsure, his back to the vehicle.

UMBERTO
(Out of frame)

We'll be in touch.

The van side-door is shut and the vehicle speeds off. Lucas starts walking in the direction of his apartment.

CUT TO:

EXT. LUCAS' APARTMENT BUILDING -- NIGHT

WIDE SHOT

Lucas enters the frame in the foreground but, before walking to the door, he stares up at the WINDOW of his own apartment. The light is on. He hesitates, not knowing what he'll say to Sonja.

INT. LUCAS' APARTMENT -- NIGHT

The front door opens slowly and a weary Lucas shuffles inside. NOISE is heard as Sonja walks over to confront him in the hallway. At first downcast, Lucas eventually lifts his eyes to confront her gaze.

SONJA
(Angry)

(Snorts) Should I even bother?

Lucas lowers his eyes after a wounded pause.

LUCAS
(Struggling)

It's… I don't know. It's a lot.

Lucas shuffles past Sonja and she glares at him in disbelief.

WIDE SHOT

Sonja follows Lucas into the living room.

SONJA

Are you kidding me? How about an explanation? You know, like a normal boyfriend would after disappearing who-knows-where for hours and then walking through the door like… like… like he just got released from jail or something.

LUCAS
(Almost whispering)

I can't. I'm sorry. Please.

SONJA
(Unimpressed)

(Sucks on teeth) Not good enough. Not even close.

Sonja begins to gather her things as she gets ready to leave.

LUCAS
(Surprised and worried)

Wait. Where are you going?

Sonja stares at him, stunned by his audacity.

SONJA
(Yelling)

Are you kidding me!? Really? You just… really?

Sonja laughs in manic frustration.

SONJA
(Lecturing)

You know Lucas. This… (Points back and forth between them) … has been a disappointment. Honestly. You don't even try anymore. And it's not like I'm demanding. (Laughs) I don't know that I can lower the bar any further. Besides. If I did you'd probably still try to limbo under it.

Grabbing her PURSE last of all, Sonja heads for the door.

VIEW ON APARTMENT ENTRY AREA

Lucas follows Sonja and she opens it halfway before he imploringly puts his hand on her arm to try and get her to stay. She quickly knocks this away though.

SONJA
(Turning to look at him)

(Pointing her finger in Lucas' face) No! You don't get to switch between indifference and concern whenever you feel like it! That's not what a relationship is! It's about giving a damn! (On the verge of crying) It's about making an effort!

LUCAS
(Aching)

Sonja. That's not how I feel. My actions, I mean… Sonja?

Sonja turns away, walking through the door.

LUCAS
(Desperate)

It's not that simple!

Lucas' words fail to have any impact as Sonja swiftly shuts the door behind her. The silence that follows her departure has the weight of calamity to it.

VIEW ON LIVING ROOM

Lucas enters the frame forlornly and looks at Biscuit the cat.

CLOSE IN ON CAT

The cat returns a blank stare.

VIEW ON BEDROOM

Lucas walks up to the doorway and stares into the darkened room.

VIEW ON APARTMENT DOOR

Suddenly the LOUD NOISE of someone bashing the door in is heard. The door is haphazardly battered open and a group of TERRIFYING THUGS start pushing their way inside. It's just a premonition though and the view snaps back to the door INTACT.

CLOSE IN

Lucas grabbing a BASEBALL BAT from the closet.

VIEW ON LIVING ROOM

Lucas enters the frame holding the baseball bat and goes to the windows to draw the BLINDS. After this is done he hesitates before heading towards the bedroom.

OVERHEAD VIEW ON LUCAS IN BED

The light in the living room is left on and the door is open so the bedroom is still dimly lit. The baseball bat is awkwardly held in Lucas' hands before he decides to place it down nearby. Finally he lies with his hands on his chest listening, before reluctantly closing his eyes. Synchronize eyes shutting with…

MATCH CUT TO:

EXT. TRAFFIC MEDIAN -- EARLY MORNING

MEDIUM SHOT

An overhead view of a woman's body lying in tall grass. This is the corpse of MS. JACOBS, an attractive woman (Late 20s) well dressed in a blouse and skirt. She looks like an office worker. No cause of death is evident and the body has a certain kind of serenity about it.

EXTREME CLOSE IN MONTAGE

The grass with the visible dew. Her lifeless hand. A DRAGONFLY settling on her before flying off.

WIDE SHOT

The area has been cordoned off by police and a tent is being erected over the dead woman. A couple POLICE OFFICERS are looking on the outskirts of the crime scene for evidence. Meanwhile, DET. GREEN and DET. SINGH approach the body. Det. Green is a butch older woman (Early 50s) with a butch haircut and Det. Singh a younger male (Mid 30s) with fastidious facial hair. Arriving at the body, Det. Singh bends down and puts on NITRATE GLOVES to examine it while Det. Green looks on with a PAPER COFFEE CUP in her hand.

DET. SINGH

It's a shame. You know, her birthday was coming up next week.

DET. GREEN

Is that so? (Sips coffee)

DET. SINGH
(Looking at Jacobs' body)

Now you're young forever. (Beat) But why?

DET. GREEN

The MPR said she disappeared two nights ago. After work. And no ostensible cause. Or at least nothing which the husband was forthcoming with.

DET. SINGH
(Looking at Det. Green)

You think it was him?

DET. GREEN
(Shaking her head)

I doubt it. In the initial report he sounded pretty shattered. (Takes a sip of her coffee) Nah, I got a hunch this is a weird one. (Beat) We'll see what the canoe makers say.

DET. SINGH
(Sighing)

Yeah, there's no obvious trauma here. Clearly she was dumped though. The indentations in the grass tell us that much. What I don't get is why anyone would leave a DB here.

DET. GREEN
(Looking off in the distance)

Maybe there was other fun to be had?

VIEW ON NEARBY ROLLERCOASTER

The old rollercoaster offers a tantalizing juxtaposition.

EXTREME WIDE SHOT

The detectives and the rollercoaster in frame.

DET. SINGH

You know, there was that dead vic who was stabbed recently. The author. And then the other one in the alley. Maybe… something bigger's going on?

DET. GREEN
(Discouraging)

Something bigger's always going on. Won't do you any good to stick your nose in it though. (Beat) That's not truffles you smell. That's the abattoir. (Finishes last of coffee)

Sinister music plays.

FADE TO RED:

INT. FIRE STATION -- EARLY MORNING

EXTREME CLOSE IN

Side of a FIRETRUCK. TRACKING shot pulls out and follows as the firetruck engages its lights and leaves the station on a call. The shot is continuous as the view shifts to…

EXT. FIRE STATION -- EARLY MORNING

The firetruck pulling away. Hold as it diminishes in frame. The sound of the sirens kicks in.

CUT TO:

EXT. INDUSTRIAL AREA -- EARLY MORNING

LONG SHOT SLOWLY ZOOMING IN

Siren noise continuous as a shackled CORPSE engulfed in gasoline fueled flames burns. The corpse is propped up and chained to a BIKE RACK while simultaneously kneeling.

CLOSE IN ON UPPER TORSO

The black flesh is melting from its skeletal face. The SOUND of the flames competes with the approaching sirens.

CLOSE IN ON HANDCUFFS

The hands of the corpse are shackled in front of it and, like the rest of the body, blackened and disintegrating.

FADE TO:

EXT. INDUSTRIAL PARK -- NIGHT

WIDE SHOT ON HIGH

A vast MURDER OF CROWS roosting in trees and on telephone wires.

FOCUS ON TWO HUMAN SILHOUETTES STANDING TOGETHER

Two men conversing inaudibly.

VIEW FROM GROUND

One of the men is Umberto and the other is an UNIDENTIFIED ASSOCIATE (Late 30's) who is imposing looking as well. Meanwhile a JOGGING PEDESTRIAN approaches them.

ANGLE EXCLUSIVELY ON JOGGING PEDESTRIAN

JOGGING PEDESTRIAN

(Respectful)

Hi. Which way's the nearest train station?

The Jogging Pedestrian's BREATH is clearly VISIBLE in the cold night air.

VIEW ON UMBERTO AND ASSOCIATE

The Associate looks at Umberto but the latter keeps his focus on the newcomer as he replies.

UMBERTO
(While gesturing)

Gilmore? Yeah. Just up the bend here and north along the road.

Umberto's breath is NOT VISIBLE.

JOGGING PEDESTRIAN

Thanks. Have a nice night.

UMBERTO
(Smiling)

You too.

VIEW ON UMBERTO

His smile holds until the jogger has left. Then it melts away and a grim look takes its place. Umberto's eyes now coolly shift from one side to the other as they focus on the Associate again.

UMBERTO
(Austere)

I hope this isn't unwelcome news about the task we gave you.

ASSOCIATE

No. Of course not. It'll take a few more days for my contact to collect it all but you'll have everything on schedule.

UMBERTO

That's good. But then that leaves the question as to why you asked for this meeting.

ASSOCIATE

Well. Some of us, not all of us, (Apologetic gesture) have concerns about the loose-end left by our late friend. Now, no one's second-guessing the lady's decision here. It's not that. But we have to explain it to the rest of our membership. And no one really knows why you're keeping the juice box in the fridge.

Umberto gives the Associate an annoyed look.

UMBERTO
(Sarcastically)

Ah. And you've decided to raise this issue with me and not her directly because… no one's "second-guessing" this decision. Right. Right. Thanks for clarifying.

ASSOCIATE
(Deferentially complaining)

You're not the only ones taking losses here.

UMBERTO
(Jeering)

Well, it's a war. What do you expect?

WIDE SHOT ON THE TWO MEN

The quiet of night counterpoints Umberto's statement.

MEDIUM SHOT

UMBERTO
(Authoritatively)

Look. He obviously wasn't involved in our late friend's mishap. We reviewed the audio of the phone records okay? Prior to our conversation with him. Meanwhile our enemies have brought in an out-of-towner and he's the only one who might be able to recognize them. So now we're grooming him. What's the problem?

ASSOCIATE

He knows things… doesn't he?

UMBERTO
(Dismissive)

He has no idea what we are.

A long pause in the conversation ensues.

ASSOCIATE
(Thoughtfully)

If he had eyes on our target… it'd just as likely the target had eyes on him. Well, more so.

UMBERTO
(Conceding)

True. But that's a much bigger problem for him than it is for us.

Umberto and the Associate share an amused look.

CUT TO:

INT. LUCAS' APARTMENT -- DAY

CLOSE IN on Lucas opening a nearly empty fridge to grab a carton of MILK. He takes this and pours it on a bowl of cereal before quickly gulping what's left and tossing the empty carton in the garbage. Hold shot as Lucas eats in the kitchen while standing.

MEDIUM SHOT IN HALLWAY

Lucas eventually enters the frame, preparing himself to leave. He's noticeably hesitant to go out.

CUT TO:

EXT. LUCAS' APARTMENT BUILDING -- DAY

Lucas appears at the front entrance, leaves the building, and exits the frame to the left.

CUT TO:

EXT. 2ND RESIDENTIAL NEIGHBORHOOD -- DAY

CLOSE IN

TRACKING shot of Lucas from behind as he is walking to a local grocery store. Eventually the kidnapper's UTILITY VAN shows up.

MEDIUM SHOT

The passenger door side of the van, adjacent to Lucas. Umberto is in the rolled down window, leaning out.

UMBERTO
(Smiling)

Vern told us you're taking some time off work.

LUCAS
(Apprehensive)

I thought it was best.

UMBERTO
(Weighing the idea)

Probably. (Beat) Hey, get in. We've got something for you.

Lucas hesitates.

CLOSE IN on Umberto

UMBERTO
(Colder)

That wasn't a request.

MEDIUM SHOT

Lucas gets in the back of the van where Kidnapper 1 and 2 are already seated. The van door is shut and the vehicle speeds off.

CUT TO:

EXT. WAREHOUSE -- DAY

The place looks semi-derelict but there are signs of lingering industry in the area. Also a couple luxury cars are parked out front. When the van shows up everyone except the DRIVER walks inside. Umberto torments Lucas with small talk.

UMBERTO

You ever work in a butcher shop? Meat packing plant?

Lucas shakes his head

UMBERTO
(Disappointed)

Oh.

CUT TO:

INT. WAREHOUSE -- DAY

Adrienne and a RETINUE of intimidating underlings. A few DEAD BODIES are lying in the immediate vicinity, victims of bladed weapons. All the dead are male and wearing dour MONASTIC style outfits. Insert a CLOSE IN shot of one of the underlings sitting and wiping their SWORD off. Lucas, Umberto, and the rest of their group now enter, drawing the attention of Adrienne.

ADRIENNE
(Playfully feigning surprise)

You found him.

UMBERTO
(Joking)

Yeah, the little guy was just wandering the streets. No collar or nothing. (Beat) We should get him chipped.

Lucas, who had previously been downcast, now notices the bodies nearby and becomes visibly squeamish and even more afraid.

ADRIENNE
(With a slight smirk)

Aw. It's okay Lucas. (Beckoning) C'mere. We just want you to look at someone.

Lucas falters to a slow pace until Umberto gives him a rough push forward. When he nears Adrienne, she puts her arm around him and leads him towards one of the bodies on the ground.

ADRIENNE
(Pointing)

That one. Do you recognize him?

Lucas reluctantly looks at the dead body. It's a man between the ages of 30 and 50. He's been stabbed repeatedly and has disfiguring wounds on his face.

ADRIENNE

You'll have to excuse the mess. We tend to be… rather enthusiastic about what we do.

LUCAS
(Mumbling)

Nuh.

ADRIENNE
(Surprised)

No?

Adrienne squeezes Lucas with the one arm she has wrapped around him in a pseudo-friendly gesture.

ADRIENNE

You sure? You didn't see him at Enoch's house? In the vicinity? (Beat) You haven't seen him at any other time, before or after?

Lucas swallows and shakes his head.

LUCAS

No.

MEDIUM SHOT

Lucas and Adrienne from behind. She drops her arm from around him and turns towards the camera, addressing Umberto.

ADRIENNE

(Sighs) Well, that's a shame. Ahhhh… (Waving her hand flippantly) Clean it all up.

CLOSE IN

Lucas turns slightly towards camera but freezes in a wince. He's expecting to die. The SOUND of approaching footsteps is heard.

UMBERTO

Hey.

MEDIUM SHOT

Lucas opens his eyes as Umberto hands him a disposable white PAINTER'S SUIT.

UMBERTO

Put that on.

Lucas looks at the outfit and then at Umberto, puzzled.

UMBERTO
(Jocular)

Come on. I'm going to show you the proper way to get rid of your victims.

FLASH VIEW

One of the underlings snapping a large sheet of translucent plastic wrapping like it was bedding. Emphasize the NOISE.

CUT TO:

EXT. AUTO REPAIR SHOP -- DAY

A SMALL CAR pulls up and parks outside. Sonja gets out.

CUT TO:

INT. AUTO REPAIR SHOP -- DAY

Werner and Royce are casually working in the GARAGE. MUSIC is playing on the radio. At first neither of them notices as Sonja enters but then they both see her. Royce approaches.

ROYCE

Hey. You can't wander back here.

SONJA
(Firmly)

I'm here to see Lucas. He's not answering me.

Before Royce can say anything, Werner takes over.

WERNER
(Pleasant)

It's Sonja right?

Werner now looks at Royce and gestures for him to go back to what he was doing before Werner returns his attention to Sonja.

WERNER
(With notable confusion)

Lucas isn't here though.

SONJA
(Exasperated)

Do you know when he'll be back?

WERNER
(Furrowing brow)

Uh, you don't know?

Sonja's eyes narrow.

WERNER

He's taking some time off.

SONJA
(Shocked)

Since when?

WERNER

Ah, two days ago.

Sonja looks away with disbelief.

SONJA
(In sheer frustration)

You asshole!

Werner realizes she isn't cursing him but is still unsure how to respond.

WERNER

I'm… sorry? (Beat) I'm sure it's just miscommunication.

SONJA
(Disgusted)

Don't defend him.

Sonja quickly exits the garage after this and Royce, wiping his hands on a rag, now walks over to Werner.

ROYCE
(After probing a tooth with his tongue)

Jeez, what a bitch.

Rather than respond to Royce's obnoxious statement, Werner eyes him with mild disgust and then turns to take care of other things. Royce laughs unsurely at this.

CUT TO:

INT. WAREHOUSE -- DAY

MEDIUM SHOT

A pile of dismembered body parts. Hold shot as Umberto speaks.

UMBERTO
(Out of frame)

Mr. D'Lambert! If you're all done puking, you can come give us a hand over here.

Kidnapper 2 chimes in now, holding separate severed hands in each of his own.

KIDNAPPER 2

I got you boss. A righty? Or a lefty?

Kidnapper 2 successively jiggles each dismembered appendage as he mentions them individually. A small amount of blood trickles off each. As the shot holds on Kidnapper 2, the laughter of several of the other men can be heard.

MEDIUM SHOT

Umberto's laughter fades as he uses a pair of PLIERS to pull out teeth from a SEVERED HEAD. He is sitting in a folding chair, with the head on his lap, going about his task like someone doing any old chore.

VIEW ON LUCAS

Lucas walks towards Umberto and the nucleus of the group. Pale faced, he's clearly been vomiting. Evidence of this, along with blood stains, ARE VISIBLE on his painter's suit.

WIDE SHOT

Several members of the group together, including Umberto, and Lucas on the far right of the frame.

UMBERTO
(Looking at Lucas and pointing out of frame)

That pile's ready to wrap over there. Just roll it up like I showed you.

VIEW ON LUCAS

Lucas convulses with a heave, putting a hand to his mouth, but doesn't puke. Then he shuffles over to do what he's been told.

MEDIUM SHOT OF ADRIENNE

She's in a distant corner of the warehouse, sitting on a folding chair, scrolling through her phone. What's striking here is how commonplace her mannerisms are, like someone commuting on a subway or waiting in an airport lounge.

CUT TO:

EXT. WAREHOUSE -- DAY

EXTREME WIDE SHOT

Fast forward to EVENING.

WIDE SHOT

The group starts leaving the warehouse, heading to their separate vehicles. Lucas, traumatized from the experience, shuffles over to the utility van he arrived in. He is no longer wearing the painter's suit.

ADRIENNE
(To Lucas)

No. You're with me.

Lucas looks at Adrienne and then at Umberto. The latter tilts his head and gestures towards Adrienne so Lucas heads towards her. Umberto's stare follows Lucas for a moment.

MEDIUM SHOT

Adrienne and Lucas around her luxury car. She opens the driver side door and starts getting in before calling to Lucas on the other side.

ADRIENNE

Make sure you're not about to drip anything on my seats before you get in.

Numbly, Lucas complies. He moves like a robot but inspects himself as thoroughly as he can. When he's done, Adrienne unlocks the door for him and he gets inside. Then the engine starts up and the car drives away. Hold shot until after it's disappeared off frame.

VIEW ON AND INSIDE CAR

Adrienne drives them through ordinary traffic. Lucas stares out the window. The details of the world are vivid but strangely distant. He's completely detached from them. Adrienne looks over and studies him for a moment before speaking.

ADRIENNE
(Seemingly caring)

You're going through quite the ordeal Lucas. But you're holding up well.

Lucas remains dazed and unresponsive.

ADRIENNE

You were asleep, living in a crude but pleasant dream. And now you're in reality. And you can never go back. (Beat) That's tough.

The car comes to a stop at a RED LIGHT and there is a MAN IN RAGS panhandling at the intersection.

VIEW ON MAN IN RAGS

ADRIENNE
(Out of frame)

As with anything else. The best thing is for you to accept it.

The Man in Rags turns to stare at Lucas.

CLOSE IN

The Man in Rags has a demonic FACE TATTOO. Unsettling music swells in. The eyes of the man are terrifying.

CUT TO:

EXT. 2ND RESIDENTIAL NEIGHBORHOOD -- NIGHT

EXTREME LONG SHOT

Adrienne's car comes around the corner at the far right of the frame and then drives forward before pulling up to a sidewalk along the near left of the frame. Its bright headlights partially obscure the occupants but something of the silhouettes of Adrienne and Lucas are visible.

INT. ADRIENNE'S CAR. 2ND RESIDENTIAL NEIGHBORHOOD -- NIGHT

WIDE SHOT

Lucas, emotionally exhausted, leaning back half-dead in his seat. Adrienne coolly scrutinizing him.

ADRIENNE

If you have a question, ask.

Lucas stirs slightly to life. Slowly glances over at Adrienne.

LUCAS

How… do I get out of this? This nightmare?

ADRIENNE

You can't fight the power of a river. You have to adapt to it. You survive. And you wait.

There is a slight pleading look in Lucas' eyes but he's unable to verbalize any response to this.

CLOSE IN ON ADRIENNE

She leans towards Lucas.

ADRIENNE
(Alluringly)

"*Finally I will drink life from your lips / And wake up from this everlasting sleep*" (Beat) That's from an ancient poet. Egyptian. (Two beats) Such… hunger. For what? A kiss.

Adrienne strokes the sleeve of Lucas' arm.

ADRIENNE

It's trust Lucas. Intimacy. Love. They all come down to trust. It's part of the essential fabric of life. It's why kissing is political… and religious… and erotic. Even animals do it. To express their interdependence. Their union. Because there's only friendship… and enmity.

Adrienne stops stroking Lucas' arm.

ADRIENNE
(Seraphic)

Should we be friends?

Lucas, wide-eyed, says nothing, but the look on his face is one of surrender. Adrienne leans in closer, dominating him.

ADRIENNE
(Quietly)

Just to warn you. I'm very cold. Like ice.

Adrienne kisses Lucas, deeply and sensuously, and the scene has the arranged quality of a renaissance painting. Hold shot until, finally, Adrienne pulls away, her mouth hovering close to his.

JUMP CUT TO:

EXT. 2ND RESIDENTIAL NEIGHBORHOOD -- NIGHT

Lucas stands and watches as Adrienne's car departs. His is a haunted look with undercurrents of longing and bewilderment. Eventually he turns towards the screen and walks off frame.

CUT TO:

INT. LUCAS' APARTMENT -- NIGHT

VIEW ON FRONT DOOR

Lucas enters with his head peeking around the door first. A look of weary expectation in his face.

VIEW ON SONJA IN THE LIVING ROOM

Anger radiates from her as she is seated facing towards the front door. Lucas enters the foreground of the frame with his back towards the camera. They are looking directly at each other. Neither speaks for a moment as the tension rises.

SONJA
(Caustically)

I'm absolutely not going to ask. I'm done asking.

LUCAS

Sonja… I, uh, I… understand why you're mad. You have every right to be. But the way things appear… it doesn't always… it's not necessarily the truth.

SONJA
(Unimpressed and rhetorical)

What the fuck does that even mean.

Lucas sighs. Sonja is almost trembling, she's so hungry for a fight. The conflict that has long been building between them is coming to its violent culmination. The NOISE of a car hitting something on the road outside the apartment briefly throws their confrontation off-balance but things quickly resume with Lucas merely glancing in the direction of the window.

LUCAS
(Searching his thoughts)

I still care about you. Maybe we can… find a way back.

Sonja springs from her chair. Furious.

SONJA
(Loudly but not quite yelling)

Now!? You want to talk about (Thinking) (?)sandbags(?)… when the water's waist deep!?

LUCAS

(Pleading)

It's us. (Softly) Our choice.

Sonja stares at Lucas as her rage is briefly warped by confusion. There's a pause between them and during this EMERGENCY SIRENS begin to be heard in the distance. Neither of them reacts to this.

LUCAS

If we trust each other. If you can trust me.

SONJA
(Scoffing)

Trust?

Sonja looks around the room and shakes her head, briefly throwing her hands up as well.

SONJA
(Speaking in flurries and jabs)

Yeah. Trust. Like what? Like, maybe, you trusting me enough to tell me what's been going on with you ever since I got back. It's like you're living on another planet.

Lucas balks. He's afraid to give an immediate answer, torn between lying and honesty, and discomfort ripples across Sonja's face as she realizes she did something she promised herself she wouldn't do; invest herself again by asking him for an explanation. Meanwhile the emergency sirens are still getting louder and Lucas reacts to this with irritation.

LUCAS
(Louder)

I just, I (Two beats) It' not really, I don't wanna… I want to keep you out of it. I'm sorry. It's too much.

Sonja stands in front of Lucas, bold and disgusted. FLASHING POLICE LIGHTS begin to bleed in through the BLINDS of the windows behind her. The emergency sirens terminate.

SONJA

For who? For you. "Sure." (Sarcastic) Or are you being aloof for my sake?

LUCAS

Sonja…

SONJA
(Loudly interrupting)

Uh uh! This was going on way before, so don't tell me that something happened suddenly to make things the way they are. Nothing happened! Nothing! It's just you. You. (In revulsion) YEW.

Sonja's words sting Lucas. He has nothing to counter them. A sense of resolve takes over her and she powers her way past him towards the bedroom. Lucas head swivels to follow her and then his attention goes back to the window. The police lights entice him to walk over, bend the blinds with his fingers, and peek outside. His face pulses in blue and red.

VIEW FROM LIVING ROOM ON BEDROOM DOOR

Sonja soon comes into frame, carrying a travel bag that has been hastily stuffed. Lucas notices her and the bag, his attention diverted from the events occurring outside.

LUCAS

You're leaving? (With slight optimism) Yes. We should leave. I mean, I won't. Not right away. But eventually.

Sonja ignores him as she focuses on collecting various small items. Lucas doesn't understand though.

LUCAS
(Sounding feverish)

And you don't need to tell anyone. We can just disappear. Vanish. As soon as I… figure out how.

SONJA
(Anger turning cold)

We're finished.

Lucas
(Surprised)

Finished?

Sonja nods. Lucas is dumbfounded. As she walks around the apartment and finishes getting ready to depart, he trails behind her in shock. Eventually he follows her to the front door where she turns around.

SONJA
(In sadness and revenge)

I loved you. Once.

Lucas, in the foreground, his back turned towards the camera, offers no protest as she exits the apartment. He even grabs the handle of the door when she leaves it open and quietly shuts it himself after a protracted gaze of longing. Lucas walks back to the living room, disappearing from the frame. Hold shot. The police lights are still pulsating.

CUT TO:

EXT. URBAN CREEK -- EVENING

WIDE SHOT

Lucas is standing at the north side of a small bridge. Thick sloping brambles line both sides of the thin snaking creek below. Its waters glow with the molten light of the setting sun. Nearby powerlines stretch over the foreground and off towards the vanishing point of the horizon. The atmosphere is funereal. Faint traffic noises coming from the east as Lucas broods over the view in front of him.

After a while, Adrienne enters the frame and leans on the railing a few feet away. She too looks out at the view but with the posture of someone admiring it. Lucas notices her but doesn't look at her. Finally he speaks.

LUCAS
(Tired and fatalistic)

I can't hide from you, can I?

ADRIENNE

Right now, we're not the ones you have to worry about.

Lucas slowly gives Adrienne a questioning look.

ADRIENNE

Last night. Outside your place. Someone else was looking for you. Not the same man who killed Enoch but… of the same persuasion. Fortunately he had an accident.

Traffic noises trace the silence that follows.

UMBERTO
(Out of frame)

You're welcome.

WIDE SHOT

Lucas and Adrienne still in frame in the foreground but the FOCUS visibly shifts to Umberto, standing guard behind them, as Lucas looks over his shoulder.

VIEW ON LUCAS AND ADRIENNE FROM BEHIND AGAIN

LUCAS

How do I know any of that's true?

ADRIENNE
(Wryly smiling)

You're starting to understand. Good.

VIEW ON UMBERTO

MEDIUM SHOT

He's still scanning the area.

VIEW ON LUCAS

CLOSE IN

LUCAS

So what happens now?

ADRIENNE

A choice. Yours. (Beat) Join us, or… (Ambiguous look)

LUCAS
(Glumly)

Or.

Lucas sighs.

ADRIENNE
(Coaxingly)

Lucas. You know what we're capable of. If we wanted that for you it would've already happened.

LUCAS
(Drained)

Yeah. I guess. (Beat) Yeah.

There's a pause in conversation before Adrienne erupts into incongruously delightful laughter.

ADRIENNE
(Nearing Lucas)

Don't be so sour. (Grabs Lucas gently by the arm) Welcome to the world. You've just been born.

Lucas allows himself to be led away by Adrienne. Umberto joins them as they all head for an SUV.

VIEW ON SETTING SUN

DISSOLVE TO:

EXT. DINER -- NIGHT

The SUV slowly drives by with Adrienne, Lucas, and Umberto.

VIEW INSIDE SUV

UMBERTO
(Driving vehicle, gazing towards diner)

I don't see them. Or their car.

ADRIENNE

They'll be there.

Adrienne looks down at her phone to check some messages.

UMBERTO
(Pulling over at the sidewalk)

Are we sending one of the others to make the hand off now?

Adrienne remains focused on her phone for a few seconds before looking up.

ADRIENNE
(Vivaciously)

I've changed my mind. Lucas is going in.

Lucas, in the backseat, perks up. Umberto looks moderately surprised but the subtext in his expression is that he's used to a certain amount of capriciousness from Adrienne.

A man comes and knocks on Adrienne's passenger side window. It's Kidnapper 1. When Adrienne rolls down the window he hands her a BULGING MANILA ENVELOPE with due deference and departs. Adrienne rolls up the window before tossing the envelope to Lucas.

LUCAS
(Confused)

What is it?

ADRIENNE

Sixty grand. In twenties.

Hearing this, Lucas reacts first by staring at the package and then staring at Adrienne.

UMBERTO

Don't get too excited.

Adrienne leans around her seat to make eye contact with Lucas.

ADRIENNE

You're just going to go inside the diner and wait. Someone will approach you. They'll use the shibboleth "Good Pilgrim" somehow. You give them the money… and they'll give you a package in return. That's it.

LUCAS

Why does that sound familiar?

Adrienne smiles at Lucas straining his memory.

LUCAS

And why me?

ADRIENNE

Well… for one…

CUT TO:

A fast cutting montage of people being brutally murdered; a man dying from piano wire, a parked car being shot up, someone bludgeoned with a claw hammer.

CUT TO:

EXT. DINER -- NIGHT

VIEW INSIDE SUV

ADRIENNE
(Vaguely)

Others are unavailable.

LUCAS
(Pointing where Kidnapper 1 came from)

But…

UMBERTO
(Cauterizing)

Maybe you don't need to fucking know?

Lucas ceases his protest. After Adrienne gestures for him to get out of the vehicle with a glance of her eyes. He opens the door and steps out.

EXT. DINER -- NIGHT

WIDE SHOT

Adrienne rolls down her window though when Lucas shuts the door so he walks over to her.

CLOSE IN

ADRIENNE

Here.

Adrienne places a METALLIC PEN in Lucas' front chest pocket and then pats it in place.

ADRIENNE

In case you need to write something down.

WIDE SHOT

Lucas now walks around the car and heads toward the diner.

VIEW INSIDE SUV

Umberto is listening to an EARPIECE. He signals to Adrienne with an Italian PERFETTO GESTURE. (Meaning: Perfect)

CUT TO:

INT. DINER -- NIGHT

The place is neat and well kept. Only one or two other patrons though. Lucas looks around before taking a seat in a vacant section. He's unable to fully suppress his nervousness but makes an extra effort when a WAITRESS comes by.

WAITRESS
(Smiling politely)

What can I get you?

LUCAS

Um. Just a coffee. Please.

WAITRESS

Sugar? Milk?

LUCAS
(Attention elsewhere)

Yeah. Both.

Sensing her presence is unwelcome, the waitress nods and leaves. Lucas sits there for a moment, fidgeting, before Det. Green walks in. She appears to notice Lucas by chance.

DET. GREEN

Dining alone?

LUCAS
(Lying, hesitantly)

I guess I've been stood up.

Det. Green makes no effort to hide the suspicion on her face.

DET. GREEN

You never know with people.

LUCAS

Uh. I suppose.

Lucas surveys the room again but then is visibly surprised as Det. Green sits down across from him.

DET. GREEN
(Almost whispering)

It's only the ones we let in who can do any real damage. Eh Lucas?

Det. Green's use of his name hits Lucas like an electric shock.

LUCAS

That's not… (Gives up) Who are you?

DET. GREEN

I'm the one collecting names. Kolmogorov. Laird. Jacobs. Although Jacob's name might not be familiar to you, the two of you did in fact speak. And actually… not too long before she died. In fact, a lot of people you've spoken to recently have ended up dead Lucas. Rather strange, don't you think?

LUCAS
(Looking sick)

I don't know why. Honestly. I don't have a fucking clue. Whoever you are.

DET. GREEN

I know that too because I'm actually very good at my job.

Det. Green flashes Lucas her BADGE and he recognizes what it is, his heart plummeting.

LUCAS
(Looking downcast)

Fuck.

In the silence that follows the waitress appears again with TWO cups of coffee.

WAITRESS
(To Det. Green)

I noticed you sit down.

DET. GREEN
(Smiling)

Of course you did darling. As always, you're impeccable.

The waitress returns Det. Green's smile warmly before departing. Lucas' agitation now bubbles up. He vibrates with it.

LUCAS
(Hissing)

So what? You want me to spill my guts? That's suicide.

Det. Green leans back, contented.

DET. GREEN
(Languidly)

Oh, you've got it all wrong Lucas. I appreciate your discretion. I want you to… continue to be a… good… pilgrim.

Lucas is flabbergasted. He looks at Det. Green with an amazement tinged in horror.

LUCAS
(Quietly)

But… what about the investigation?

Det. Green chuckles and takes a sip of her coffee.

DET. GREEN

The police don't even know about you.

LUCAS
(Aggressively objecting)

You're the police.

DET. GREEN
(Smirking)

When it suits me.

Lucas can only offer a weak gesture of defeat in response to this and Det. Green enjoys her coffee a moment longer, holding it close to her mouth, before speaking.

DET. GREEN

Okay. Hand it over.

Lucas attempts to pass the package stealthily under the table but Det. Green waves this off and beckons for him to just put the package on top of it. Sheepishly, Lucas does so and, after taking it, Det. Green slides a much SMALLER PACKAGE towards him that she was keeping in her pocket.

DET. GREEN

That's it. (Pointing at Lucas' undrunk coffee) I got you. You can go.

Slowly, Lucas gets up and then pauses beside the table.

LUCAS
(Unsure)

Do you have any (?)messages(?) for me? For them?

Det. Green shakes her head with a perplexed expression on her face. She pulls out her phone then and, seeing her ignoring him, Lucas leaves.

CUT TO:

EXT. DINER -- NIGHT

Lucas rapidly walks, and then jogs, over to the SUV. Opening the door, he gets in.

VIEW INSIDE SUV

ADRIENNE

So it went pretty good.

Lucas nods.

ADRIENNE

Alright.

Adrienne stretches her hand out to Lucas in the back seat. Quickly, Lucas hands over the package. Adrienne takes it but then holds her hand out again and Lucas is puzzled.

ADRIENNE
(Jokingly quoting Vladimir Putin in perfect Russian)

"Give me back my pen."

LUCAS

Huh?

UMBERTO

Give the lady her pen back.

With a look of suspicion on his face, Lucas complies.

CUT TO:

EXT. ADRIENNE'S URBAN COMPOUND -- NIGHT

WIDE SHOT

Two SUVs approach the front gate. One contains Adrienne, Umberto, and Lucas. The other has Kidnapper 1 as well as some other THUGS in it. The gate opens automatically and then closes after they both drive inside.

EXT. COMPOUND COURTYARD -- NIGHT

Both SUVs park near the front entrance.

INT. ADRIENNE'S URBAN COMPOUND -- NIGHT

Although aesthetically faultless, the décor is fairly Spartan except for some odd abstract sculptures. Works that might be described as hyper-cubist or biomechanical. The lighting it also somewhat unusual, creating a slightly ethereal atmosphere. The camera floats through a cross section of the space before settling on the main doors where a GUARD is sitting on a stool with a P-90 ASSAULT RIFLE on his knees. A large FLAT SCREEN MONITOR near him shows the progress of the group outside from multiple camera angles. Eventually they reach the door and enter the frame proper. ADRIENNE arrives first, acknowledging the GUARD with a nod, and several of those who follow do likewise in their own individual ways. At the same time, a SULTRY WOMAN (Late 40s) in an alluring dress arrives and greets Adrienne with obsequious cheek kissing.

SULTRY WOMAN

You're a fortress to us all. Never forget how proud everyone is of you. Especially…

She sees Lucas in the midst.

SULTRY WOMAN
(Eying Lucas but speaking to Adrienne)

What's this?

ADRIENNE
(Touching Lucas warmly)

Our own Lucas. Fresh from initiation.

SULTRY WOMAN
(Smiling at Adrienne)

Quite the morsel. Which reminds me, I was hoping we could share a drink later.

ADRIENNE

Of course.

SULTRY WOMAN

Good. I have… well, we'll talk tonight. I simply want to make sure you're getting thorough updates on the situation with… our inventory.

ADRIENNE

Thank you. Your diligence is always appreciated.

SULTRY WOMAN
(Gently downplaying herself)

I only aspire to be a dutiful daughter.

Here the Sultry Woman walks off in one direction while Adrienne walks off in another and the rest of the group that arrived settles in or leaves with various personal objectives.

CENTER VIEW ON LUCAS

As the group starts to fragment, Lucas stands watching them drift away. He is unsure of what to do.

VIEW ON ADRIENNE

A few feet ahead of Lucas, she realizes he isn't with her anymore and turns slightly to look for him. Making eye contact, she curls her index finger in a beckoning gesture.

CUT TO:

INT. COMPOUND STUDY -- NIGHT

Fine sensuous woodwork and velvet tones provide a warm contrast to the minimalist and monochromatic entrance space outside. Shelves of old books and INTRIGUING ARTIFACTS abound. Adrienne enters. She smiles at someone out of frame in front of her and then proceeds to a desk. There she begins looking at DIAGRAMS, some of which are laid in small piles and others scrolled up.

ADRIENNE
(Calling to Lucas behind her)

Don't be shy.

VIEW FACING LUCAS

Lucas enters the room. He's taken aback by something he sees outside the frame though.

VIEW ON ADRIENNE

She looks up from the desk while still leaning over it. Then the camera PANS right to a view of her CONCUBINE. The attractive concubine is lying fully naked in a reclined medical chair while blood is drawn from her by a TALL IV MACHINE.

WIDE SHOT

Adrienne and the Concubine in the middle ground with Lucas, back to screen, in the foreground. Adrienne gives Lucas a reassuring, albeit half-impatient, look and Lucas shuffles closer. His mix of discomfort and interest in the naked Concubine endures even as he turns his back to her and focuses on what Adrienne wants to show him. Meanwhile the rising and falling of the Concubine's bare chest is noticeable.

MEDIUM SHOT

Adrienne and Lucas standing at the desk. Taking out the diner package from an INNER JACKET POCKET, Adrienne opens this and pours out a pair of CATHAR CROSS PENDANTS from inside.

VIEW ON ADRIENNE

She raises an eyebrow.

VIEW ON LUCAS

He doesn't understand.

MEDIUM SHOT

Adrienne picks up one of the pendants and holds it between her thumb and index finger.

ADRIENNE

A fob.

LUCAS
(Murmuring)

A fob.

ADRIENNE
(Enunciating)

A KEY fob.

LUCAS

Oh.

ADRIENNE

This one's for you, tinker tailor.

Adrienne places it in Lucas' hand and presses his hand closed.

LUCAS
(Weighing his words)

What… am I doing with it?

ADRIENNE
(Enthusiastic)

Well, if you thought the diner was fun… (Smiles) We're going to infiltrate the prison of a paramilitary religious order. And… you're coming with.

Lucas absorbs the news with a pained expression but recovers.

LUCAS

Isn't that… absurd? I'm not a covert, mercenary, whatever.

ADRIENNE

Oh, you won't have to do much. But we can only put two people in and our specialist, who you'll be accompanying, needs at least one other person to assist him. And although you can't recall anyone suspicious who you think might be Enoch's killer, it's possible you could recognize them if you saw them. Which would be good for this task since…

LUCAS
(Morosely)

He might be there.

ADRIENNE

Exactly.

Lucas pauses, and then laughs in manic surrender.

LUCAS

Alright. Sure. Par for the course. But, uh (Beat) Can I get, like, a disguise for this thing?

ADRIENNE
(Cheerfully)

Oooo… why not.

Adrienne pats Lucas on the cheek in an affection manner and then turns to leave, tilting her head to indicate he should follow her. Lucas gives the pendant a slight toss in the air as he prepares to obey but then notices the naked Concubine again. She is looking him directly in the eyes and he stares at her for a moment blankly before hurriedly going after Adrienne. Hold shot on Concubine as her gaze follows his departure.

DISSOLVE TO:

INT. COMPOUND COMMON AREA -- DAY, NIGHT, DAY

Begin a montage of scenes showing the group preparing for their mission. These include:

(1) Lucas being introduced to HERODOTUS, an older (Mid 40s) field agent for the group. They meet while being fitted for the monastic outfits they'll need to wear during the infiltration. Herodotus is having his outfit adjusted by a third party when the montage cuts into him and Lucas in mid conversation.

HERODOTUS

We'll arrive in separate vehicles.

LUCAS

Makes sense.

HERODOTUS

You'll go in first. Follow your route. And we'll "meet" at the end.

LUCAS

Right. To do… what?

HERODOTUS
(Impassively)

Speak with someone.

FADE WHITE:

(2) Lucas being shown things on a map by Kidnapper 1 without speech or ambient audio. Focus on the expressions of his face and his increasingly concerned reactions.

FADE WHITE:

(3) Lucas and Umberto sitting down together. Umberto places a TINY VIAL of amber hued poison on the table in front of them.

LUCAS

Is that all?

UMBERTO

Also… there's the DNA for their security system.

LUCAS
(Grumbling)

Great. So you want a sample.

UMBERTO

We already took it.

LUCAS
(Puzzled)

How?

Umberto motions plucking a hair from Lucas' head with a mocking smile. Lucas is unamused.

DISSOLVE TO:

EXT. COMPOUND COURTYARD -- EVENING

WIDE DOWNWARD ELEVATED SHOT

The sound of a dog barking in the distance can be heard as Lucas, Herodotus, Adrienne, and Umberto exit the main building of the urban compound. Two BLACK JEEPS are parked nearby.

MEDIUM LEVEL SHOT

Umberto and Herodotus take time to share a smoke as Lucas and Adrienne speak. Lucas has dyed hair and a new haircut. Adrienne fusses over Lucas' monk outfit.

ADRIENNE
(Satisfied)

You're practically Vatican ready.

LUCAS

I feel ridiculous.

ADRIENNE

Well, don't forget these.

After saying this, she puts a pair of VINTAGE 80s prescription style SHIELD GLASSES on him. Lucas scowls.

ADRIENNE

You wanted a disguise. But maybe… wait until after driving.

WIDE SHOT

Lucas takes the glasses off and Herodotus tosses the butt of his cigarette away. Lucas gets a better look at both the jeeps.

LUCAS

They're identical.

HERODOTUS

That's their preference.

Herodotus gets in the lead jeep and waits for Lucas to get in his own. Lucas goes to the driver side door but then calls out to Adrienne and Umberto.

LUCAS

This could still go off the rails.

Adrienne and Umberto share a glance before Umberto takes a long drag and then responds to Lucas.

UMBERTO
(Loudly)

Just remember what Mishima said. "*When faced with a choice between living and dying, choose death.*"

Lucas stonily absorbs this and turns away to get into his jeep.

WIDE DOWNWARD ELEVATED SHOT

The two jeeps depart the compound as Adrienne and Umberto watch. Then a CONVOY of SUVs pull up. Adrienne and Umberto get in the passenger sides of separate vehicles and the CONVOY follows the jeeps at a distance.

CUT TO:

Aerial highway shots as the pair of JEEPS travel to their rural destination. The SUV convoy in separate shots. Use music to gradually build tension.

LEVEL WIDE SHOT

At the end of the highway sequence, Herodotus slows his jeep down so Lucas' can take the lead.

CUT TO:

EXT. PRISON OF THE VIGILANTS -- TWILIGHT

EXTREME LONG SHOT RUSHING FORWARD

The outside of the Prison of the Vigilants is hypermodern and minimalist; like a giant quartz rhombus. Its very existence is alien. Surreal. Located in the basin of a rural mountain valley, the building is introduced through a rapid forward dolly shot, but one that's gradually losing speed, as it's overtaken by the two jeeps appearing from the bottom of the frame and following the road leading through the frame's center. The roaring noise of the jeeps' passage mixes with the forceful music that has been continuously building since the highway sequence. The roar fades as the music peaks. Lucas' jeep commands a significant lead but both jeeps shrink as they converge on the prison.

CUT TO:

EXT. PRISON GATE -- TWILIGHT

WIDE DOWNWARD ANGLE

Lucas' jeep going through the gate after a guard lets him through. The gate shutting. Herodotus' jeep arriving.

CUT TO:

WIDE SHOT

Lucas' jeep entering the underground parking lot.

INT. UNDERGROUND PARKING LOT

EXTREME WIDE SHOT

The underground parking lot is large and ultramodern. Lucas' jeep arrives and parks near the MAIN DOORS. These are flanked by BORED GUARDS in BLACK KEVLAR.

WIDE ON DOORS

Lucas enters the hospital-emergency-like entrance and is still visible through the LARGE WINDOWS when he's inside.

CUT TO:

INT. PRISON RECEPTION AREA

The SECURITY ADMINISTRATOR at the desk indifferently notes Lucas' approach. Lucas runs his key fob against a scanner and his information appears on the Administrator's display panel. A ROBOTIC mounted THERMAL IMAGINING SCANNER, reminiscent of an insect's compound eye, scans Lucas and the heat imagery comes up on the administrator's display panel. Then a guard gestures for Lucas to provide a blood sample for a "hand-stamping" INJECTOR APPARATUS. After Lucas has his hand stamped by the machine, video of blood cells under ELECTRON MICROSCOPY appears on the display panel along with DNA graphics including NUCLEOBASE diagrams and a GENOME SEQUENCE. The style of these visuals are not contemporary though and allude to the technology having been in long use and not updated. Having provided them with all they require, the Administrator waves Lucas through.

LUCAS

Thanks.

CUT TO:

INT. PRISON HALLWAY

Lucas walking through a bare inimical corridor, being cautious not to reveal the fraud of his adopted persona. Pointedly not looking towards two MONKS who pass by him in the opposite direction. The sound of all their footsteps, echoing.

CUT TO:

INT. STAIRWELL ENTRANCE

WIDE SHOT

Lucas approaches from the foreground and looks at the wide stairwell leading to a dark area below. He uses his key fob to unlock an automatically opening BULLETPROOF GLASS DOOR and begins his descent.

CUT TO:

INT. PRISON UNDERCROFT

Making his way down the stairs, Lucas arrives at a much older area which the newer architecture was built on top of. Here the environment takes on the appearance of an early 19TH century prison with brick and wrought iron workmanship. It's like the building above is meant to protect the world from the haunted structure underneath it.

Lucas continues his forward incursion and the hallway now has CELLS with heavy BARRED DOORS that have been modified with bullet proof glass casing. Not stopping, he notices that these cells house MUTANT CLONES, identical looking prisoners afflicted with varying REALISTIC physical abnormalities. Eventually he stops in front of one of these when he encounters a prisoner, a PSYCHOTIC CLONE, speaking to themselves. When they notice Lucas in turn, they shamble to the door and address him.

PSYCHOTIC CLONE
(Creepy and unhinged)

Thare was waarr in heaven, oh yessss, and the rebels, the defeated, wurr (Agitatedly pointing downwards) casht to earth. (Beat passes before he makes a crashing sound with his mouth) No longer glory-us and etheer-re-al, they dwhelled in the rue-inous flesh. They inhabited the beasts… ALLLL of them. The swine of course. And the ssserpent. (Nodding before looking upwards) Infesting the air, they took possession; and they crept into the har-tsss of men. (Long pause) So… where are they now? (His eyes almost spasm as he succumbs to deranged mirth)

Lucas backs away from the cell and continues on his route.

CUT TO:

INT. 1ST UNDERCROFT HALLWAY

LONG SHOT

Lucas enters the frame and sees a monk standing in the distance. He hesitates and the monk remains still. Unsure, he begins to move closer. He tries to hide his caution. Eventually the monk gestures for Lucas to hurry up.

MEDIUM SHOT

It's Herodotus. The two men come together and whisper.

LUCAS
(Hushed)

I should be good.

HERODOTUS
(Hushed)

The longer we stay the less likely that's true.
Come. She should be just around the corner.

The two men begin to walk together. Lucas furtively glances at the dome of a surveillance camera on the roof.

LUCAS
(Hushed)

Your source. The one who works inside here. Can't they help us?

HERODOTUS
(Hushed)

They won't. We don't even know who they are. We trade the information anonymously. Now… quiet.

Lucas and Herodotus walk around a corner.

EXT. THE SIBYL'S CHAMBER

An incongruously open space with eerie soundproofing in the form of WALLS of black rubber spikes. The emaciated SIBYL, ivory and haggard, is hanging from the ceiling by a single cable connected to her wrist shackles. Another cable meanwhile stretches from the ground and is connected to her ankle shackles. She is suspended in the air like a lunar sliver in the void.

Lucas and Herodotus enter but when Herodotus sees her, he talks to Lucas in an aside first.

HERODOTUS

I'll speak to The Sibyl alone. Go and keep a watch in the hall. We'll proceed to the artifact when I'm done.

LUCAS

Alright.

Lucas turns to leave but Herodotus stops him with a hand.

HERODOTUS

If you see a security team headed here, cry the warning.

Herodotus glares at Lucas to emphasize his seriousness.

WIDE SHOT

Herodotus approaching The Sibyl. He nears her with reverence but she doesn't raise her drooping head until he begins to speak.

HERODOTUS
(Gingerly)

Sister? (Beat) Sister?

THE SIBYL
(Stirring weakly)

Who?

HERODOTUS

One of the family.

THE SIBYL
(Sighing)

Ah. She did not forget me.

HERODOTUS

No my lady. But I am afraid we cannot get you out.

THE SIBYL

Of course not. And yet you came.

HERODOTUS

We must know if the lineage has been compromised. The inquisition has renewed itself against us.

THE SIBYL

The elder covenant is still unbroken. (Gasps) Not by me.

Herodotus nods as he eyes The Sibyl sorrowfully. He is downcast for a moment before raising his head again.

HERODOTUS

Then let me end your pain my poor sister.

MEDIUM SHOT

The Sybil hanging above Herodotus.

THE SIBYL

So be it.

CLOSE IN

Herodotus bends down to retrieve two hidden items from his boot. One is a long thin BLADE, the other is the TINY VIAL of amber hued poison. He stands up and twists off the vial's cap. After dipping the tip of the blade in the liquid inside, he recaps it and takes a deep breath. He seems to have doubts.

THE SIBYL
(Hoarsely)

Do not forsake me now brother.

Herodotus steels his resolve and stabs The Sibyl in the ribcage in a manner that mimics the iconography of Christ being stabbed by the spear of Longinus. The Sibyl lets out a loud EXHALE.

CUT TO:

INT. 2ND UNDERCROFT HALLWAY

A group of MONKS hurriedly heading towards The Sibyl's chamber. The leader of these is FATHER MALACHI (Late 40s) a grim, imposing figure. He marches ahead as three others follow.

CUT TO:

INT. THE SIBYL'S CHAMBER

Herodotus reacts as the monks trample in by immediately slashing at Father Malachi with his blade. Father Malachi dodges this, flinging himself aside, but then a less spry JUNIOR MONK is punctured once before Herodotus backs off himself. At first the Junior Monk is puzzled but then horrified. The same realization also dawns on the face of an OLDER MONK.

OLDER MONK
(Loudly)

Poison!

CUT TO:

Lucas is looking in another direction distractedly when a shout from the Older Monk snaps his attention towards The Sibyl's chamber.

OLDER MONK
(Out of Frame)

POISON!

Lucas takes a few steps towards the chamber as the NOISE of the conflict escalates. Doubt springs on his face however and, after pausing a moment, he flees in the opposite direction.

CUT TO:

INT. THE SIBYL'S CHAMBER

CLOSE IN ON FLOOR

Herodotus' blade bounces across the floor, knocked out of his hands by unseen means.

WIDE SHOT

The monks wrestling a standing Herodotus. At first he resists in an attempt to get away but, as the apparent hopelessness of his situation becomes manifest, he struggles to grab the vial of poison.

CLOSE IN

Herodotus has the vial of poison in his hand and, fighting against the monks trying to drag him to the ground, he gets it in his mouth and bites down. The SOUND of the vial being broken between his jaws is heard. The monks then force him to the floor before turning him over. He's breathing very hard.

CLOSE IN ON FATHER MALACHI

The leader of the monks, in the scrum and leaning over, glowers at Herodotus as he realizes that the man has managed to commit suicide. Controlled anger and frustration are evident.

EXTREME CLOSE IN ON HERODOTUS

The life is rapidly draining out of him.

CUT TO:

INT. STAIRWELL ENTRANCE

Lucas anxiously making his way up the stairs, rising into view from these in the middle ground. Then exiting frame.

CUT TO:

INT. PRISON RECEPTION AREA

Lucas making his way past the guards, with a thin veneer of false calm, and out into the parking lot.

CUT TO:

INT. UNDERGROUND PARKING LOT

Lucas getting into his jeep and haphazardly driving away.

EXT. PRISON GATES -- NIGHT

DOWNWARD ANGLED WIDE SHOT

The gate takes an agonizingly long time to open. Once it is though, Lucas' jeep lurches past.

CUT TO:

EXT. VALLEY HIGHWAY SECTION 1 -- NIGHT

Lucas' jeep racing down the road.

INT. LUCAS' JEEP

Lucas is constantly checking in his REAR VIEW MIRROR to see if he's being followed. After a couple glances he thinks he's in the clear but then the HIGH BEAMS of two PURSUING JEEPS lets him know he hasn't made a clean getaway. AUDIO CUE with a sound effect like synthesized thunder underscores this. Then the engine ROARS as Lucas puts his foot to the gas pedal.

EXT. VALLEY HIGHWAY SECTION 2 -- NIGHT

EXTREME WIDE SHOT

A perpendicular shot of the road with Lucas' jeep racing by, then the pursuing jeeps, and finally, significantly later, the SUVs that contain Adrienne and Umberto.

EXT. VALLEY INDUSTRIAL AREA -- NIGHT

Lucas' jeep makes a turnoff. He's trying to lose his pursuers. CLASSIC MO-TOWN begins playing.

INT. MALACHI'S JEEP -- NIGHT

In pursuit of Lucas, the jeep is bumping up and down as it rushes through a spot of rough terrain. Continuous audio of the Mo-Town song from the previous scene but here the music is coming from the jeep's radio. Malachi hits a dog while chasing Lucas' vehicle but doesn't slow down.

EXT. VALLEY INTERSECTION -- NIGHT

Lucas crashes his jeep dramatically but doesn't roll it. Injured from hitting the steering wheel, Lucas nevertheless remains cognizant and quickly ditches the car. As he flees the scene though it's clear he's seriously injured and he staggers through the street as someone would with the wind knocked out of them.

EXT. AQUARIUM SHOWROOM -- NIGHT

EXTREME WIDE SHOT

The large generic building is only partially illuminated by the electric lights in the vicinity. Lucas enters the right of the frame and goes around the side of the building to try and find a way in. He's desperate for somewhere to hide.

INT. AQUARIUM SHOWROOM -- NIGHT

WIDE SHOT

Various large AQUARIUM TANKS, filled with water but empty of everything else, rest on elevated stands in individual islands of light provided by overhead illumination. A single tank however in the center of the frame has a lone fish in it.

CLOSE IN

The fish is a PIRANHA. It does very little. Then the SOUND of breaking glass is heard.

MEDIUM SHOT

Lucas clearing the glass from a broken window before climbing inside the building. After falling to the floor, he picks himself up and leaves the frame with obvious hurt.

EXT. AQUARIUM SHOWROOM -- NIGHT

Father Malachi arrives in his jeep and parks near the front entrance.

INT. MALACHI'S JEEP -- NIGHT

Father Malachi reaches in his glove box and takes out the Custom Balaclava he used while killing Enoch and the other victim.

CLOSE IN

Malachi hesitates before putting the balaclava back in the glove box and grabbing a DESERT EAGLE handgun instead.

EXT. AQUARIUM SHOWROOM -- NIGHT

Father Malachi gets out looks at the other jeep with his associates arriving before he heads for the trunk of his vehicle. The two monks from the other jeep exit and appear with M4 CARBINE ASSAULT RIFLES.

FATHER MALACHI
(Authoritatively)

Hold the others off. I'm going inside.

The two monks do as they're told, taking up defensive positions to ambush their adversaries. Meanwhile, Father Malachi goes to the trunk of his jeep and pulls out a CUSTOM SHOTGUN, triggering a foreboding AUDIO CUE.

CUT TO:

INT. AQUARIUM SHOWROOM -- NIGHT

Lucas attempting to move stealthily as he looks for a place to hide away from the main aquarium display area. Then he hears someone out of frame kick the front doors a couple times before a SHOTGUN BLAST sounds and the SOUND of a door being bashed aside. Lucas goes from noticeable trepidation to outright fear. He strains to hear, trying to pinpoint the location of the person hunting him when he's startled by ECHOING SEMI-AUTOMATIC GUNFIRE sounding in bursts. A battle has begun.

WIDE SHOT

Father Malachi, his shotgun raised, searching the showroom with mercenary professionalism. He nears the area where Lucas is hiding when the NOISE of a window breaking is heard. Malachi pivots and aims in that general direction as he gradually begins to approach. Meanwhile, the crackle of semi-automatic gunfire is still being heard outside.

WIDE SHOT

Adrienne, BLADE in hand and almost a silhouette, appearing in a door frame. With spectacular speed she dodges in a balletic fashion just as Father Malachi unloads several rounds at her.

MEDIUM SHOT

Father Malachi firing once and then pausing.

FATHER MALACHI
(Yelling)

Come on you blood drinking bitch! I've got thirty pellets of silver for you!

MEDIUM SHOT

Lucas watching as Father Malachi walks past his position, the latter's back turned to him. Father Malachi fires again and the SOUND of one of the aquarium tanks exploding is heard.

MEDIUM SHOT

Father Malachi scoffing with his gun raised.

FATHER MALACHI
(Taunt)

Running out of thralls!?

WIDE SHOT

Adrienne standing in partial light. She is supernaturally still.

MEDIUM SHOT

Father Malachi preparing to fire. He's hit with a tackle by Lucas though. The gambit doesn't work however as Father Malachi is barely stunned and he unloads a round on Lucas, hitting him in the UPPER LEG and knocking him to the floor.

MEDIUM ANGLE ON FATHER MALACHI

He's weighing whether to execute Lucas outright when Adrienne rushes him from the darkness. She backhands his shotgun out of his grip while simultaneously slashing his neck and sundering his clavicle in a single stroke. Clear view of wound. This action sequence furthermore uses an AGGREGATE COMPOSITION of successive frames with an accompanying WARPED audio effect. Adrienne's eyes meanwhile are as eldritch black as the void and her face contorted with animalistic ferocity.

ADRIENNE
(Voice reverberating with sinister occult power)

{{{O O P S}}}

MEDIUM SHOT

After her jeering remark, Adrienne begins to feed on Father Malachi, chugging blood from his neck while making nausea inducing gulping noises and physically convulsing with the satiation of her dark hunger. This goes on a moment before she gets her fill and lets Malachi's partially raised corpse drop completely to the floor. With blood running down her chin, she touches her mouth and delicately licks her lips before turning towards where Lucas is off frame.

MEDIUM SHOT

Lucas sprawled but half erect on the floor. His leg is heavily wounded and blood is pooling around him. He's dazed but looking upwards as Adrienne's shadow falls over him.

LUCAS
(Weakly)

You're a…

MEDIUM SHOT

Adrienne looking down with black eyes and a demonic smile.

ADRIENNE
(Lusciously)

{{{YES}}}

WIDE SHOT

Lucas and Adrienne both in frame. Lucas making a renewed effort to put pressure on his wound but very half-heartedly.

LUCAS
(Fading in and out)

I think The Sibyl's dead. And Herod… (Sighs) You… what's it like?

CLOSE IN ON ADRIENNE'S FACE

ADRIENNE
(Exalting)

{{{POWER}}}

CLOSE IN

Lucas heaves slightly and stomach bile dribbles from his mouth. He notices this but is in too much shock to be embarrassed. His focus returns to Adrienne.

LUCAS
(Childlike)

I'm afraid.

VIEW ON ADRIENNE

Despite her overwhelmingly predatory aura, something in her seems to soften slightly at his words.

MEDIUM SHOT

Adrienne bends down and slits Lucas' throat as the expression of his face suggests a kind of nihilistic communion. The blood flows in a stream down his neck. Adrienne stands up while still looking down at him.

WIDE SHOT

Umberto with a SCOPED RIFLE at the front door, something of the exterior outdoors visible as well.

LONG SHOT

Adrienne looks in Umberto's direction beyond camera and begins to walk towards him. When she reaches one of the aquarium tanks though she pauses.

CLOSE IN

Adrienne dangling a bloodied hand over the water. A drop of blood from her index finger falls in.

VIEW ON BLOOD DROPLET

The blood dissolves gracefully in the water. Hold shot.

DISSOLVE TO:

EXT. MIST FILLED TROPICAL JUNGLE -- EVENING

The SOUNDS of nocturnal jungle wildlife swell as the camera TRACKS forward through a lush but traversable section of the jungle floor. Simultaneous SLOW ZOOM on a small red object in the distance. The object is moving.

MEDIUM SHOT

Zooming in, the object is revealed to be a placenta covered as newborn. The SOUND of the child's crying begins to predominate. The infant, kicking and fidgeting weakly is a baby girl with a DEFORMED LEG.

CLOSE IN

The child has been abandoned on an ANT HILL. The ants are beginning to envelop her. She continues crying.

EXTREME CLOSE IN

We see her face. Her closed eyes. Her cries are piercing. Heart rending. The ants are small but monstrous in detail.

SLOW DISSOLVE TO BLACK:

The sound of the crying from the abandoned child continues. Hold black. The crying stops abruptly. The credits start rolling.

THE END

www.ingramcontent.com/pod-product-compliance
Lightning Source LLC
LaVergne TN
LVHW050324160826
845677LV00014B/3529

* 9 7 9 8 3 5 5 7 1 3 8 1 2 *